'Do you v...... ... ...n friends?'

He looked de........................t for her as thou...

As Jemima gave herself up to the magic of it, she thought that this was her answer. There *was* chemistry between them.

But raised voices outside on the seafront were breaking into their absorption in each other. 'Jack! Are you up there? There's been an explosion on a trawler five miles out.'

'Don't go!' she choked.

'What? You of all people should know better than to say that.'

'I of all people know what can happen to those who man the lifeboats!' she flung back.

'Maybe, but we'll talk about it when I get back. I have to go.'

If you get back, she thought wretchedly. Terror would be her companion every time a doctor was needed on the lifeboat, because she was in love with Jack. She wasn't going to be able to cope with it.

Abigail Gordon loves to write about the fascinating combination of medicine and romance from her home in a Cheshire village. She is active in local affairs and is even called upon to write the script for the annual village pantomime! Her eldest son is a hospital manager and helps with all her medical research. As part of a closeknit family, she treasures having two of her sons living close by and the third one not too far away. This also gives her the added pleasure of being able to watch her delightful grandchildren growing up.

Recent titles by the same author:

THE ELUSIVE DOCTOR
SAVING SUZANNAH
EMERGENCY REUNION
THE NURSE'S CHALLENGE

EMERGENCY RESCUE

BY
ABIGAIL GORDON

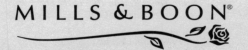

MILLS & BOON®

MILLS & BOON and MILLS & BOON with the Rose Device are registered trademarks of the publisher.

First published in Great Britain 2002
Harlequin Mills & Boon Limited,
Eton House, 18-24 Paradise Road, Richmond, Surrey TW9 1SR

© Abigail Gordon 2002

ISBN 0 263 83067 5

Set in Times Roman 10½ on 12 pt.
03-0502-50492

Printed and bound in Spain
by Litografia Rosés, S.A., Barcelona

CHAPTER ONE

JEMIMA PENROSE tightened her grip on the steering-wheel as the harbour came into view. The doors of the lifeboat house were open and visitors to the quaint Cornish town were lined up along the promenade, waiting. For what, she wasn't sure, but she could make a guess.

The noticeboard at the top of the sloping concrete ramp had the answer. It said that at six o'clock that evening there would be a launching of the craft that never failed to catch the imagination of the general public because of its associations with danger, courage and the raw forces of nature.

Why, for goodness' sake, hadn't she taken the back road? she thought miserably. It would have been more sensible. Sooner or later she would have had to drive past this place, but not on the very moment of her return.

Drive on, she told herself, and wondered why she did the opposite by availing herself of a space on a parking area down the nearest side street and then going to join the waiting crowd.

Obviously there was no emergency. Tonight's launch was for the benefit of visitors. When the lifeboat was called out on a distress signal there were no previous announcements. The crew dropped everything and came running and within minutes they were off.

As she leaned against the metal rail that separated the seafront from the ramp, Jemima told herself that maybe it was best that she faced up to it now, instead of later. The two years that she'd been away from this place had helped her to batten down the horror, and now there was just grief to cope with.

The sea today, in early October, was incredibly blue and very calm. High summer had gone but there was a mellowness about the scene that brought a lump to her throat.

Until a wild winter's night two years ago she would never have believed that she would end up running away from the small coastal town where she'd been born. Yet she had, and it had only been her mother's plea that she come home for the wedding that had brought Jemima back to Rockhaven.

There was a sudden buzz of interest amongst those waiting, and as Jemima looked up from the flurry of fine golden sand at her feet she saw why. The Severn class lifeboat was moving slowly down the ramp towards the harbour bed, which the receding tide had left dry, and from there it would go out into the mighty Atlantic, the only urgency on this occasion being that the crew should be back in time for supper.

Jemima felt her nerve ends tighten like the tow rope attached to a weather-beaten Jeep that was pulling the boat towards the sea. Her grip on the metal rail in front of her had tightened too, just as it had on the steering-wheel of her car when she'd seen the open doors of the lifeboat house.

There were three of the crew on board, two helmsmen and the coxswain. They were smiling at the interested onlookers and as they passed one of them called down laughingly to a tall figure walking down the ramp beside the brightly coloured craft.

It was a voice she'd heard countless times before, and never more memorably than on that horrendous night when Bill Stennet had bellowed above the roar of the storm. 'Man overboard!'

Just the mere sound of it was sending her back in time to the worst gale she'd ever seen. Walls of water twenty feet high had swept down onto the Severn every few seconds as the lifeboat had tried to get near the fishing vessel that had been on the point of sinking.

It hadn't been her first trip as the only female member of the crew, but it had certainly been her last. As it had been for her father, Stephen Penrose, the coxswain. The difference was that she'd had a choice whether she sailed with them again and he hadn't.

The thunder of the waves was in her ears again. Like huge beasts of prey, grey and foam-tipped, they'd tossed the lifeboat about in the seething cauldron they'd created and she was slipping down into it, as she had done so many other times in her nightmares.

As her legs went slack beneath her the last thing Jemima saw was the surprised blue eyes of the man who was walking beside the lifeboat, and then everything became hazy.

She wasn't aware that he'd leapt over the rail and was telling those who were crowding around her, 'I'm a doctor. Will you stand back, please?'

Neither did she hear her father's old friend Bill Stennet, say in gruff alarm, 'Why, it's Jemima! Where has *she* appeared from? What's wrong with her, Jack?'

'I'm not sure,' Jack Trelawney told him. 'Probably just a faint—she's coming round already. Maybe she collapsed from exhaustion or stress, or she's sickening for something.'

The older man gave a dubious nod.

'Aye, or else she was seein' something that we weren't.'

Keen eyes, as blue as the sea that was skipping back towards the harbour entrance, were asking for an explanation and the lifeboat crewman obliged.

'Jemima? Dr Jemima Penrose? Daughter of the late

Stephen and soon to become a relative of yours by marriage?'

Jack Trelawney gave a slow whistle of surprise as his
glance went over the figure at his feet. So this long-limbed,
pale-skinned brunette, whose head was resting on his knee
as she tried to focus on him, was the prodigal daughter.
The long-gone offspring of the woman that his father intended to marry. Who had left her mother to cope alone
with widowhood and had hidden herself away for the last
two years in some hospital in the Midlands.

Was she ill? he wondered. Suffering from some kind of
weakness? Or was it like old Bill has just said, that she'd
been hit by a blast from the past?

The same blue eyes that had been watching her as she'd
crumpled onto the seafront were looking down at her now,
Jemima thought weakly as her vision righted itself.

The face they belonged to was becoming clearer and she
saw that above them golden brows were raised as if in some
sort of surprise, and below the bright blue orbs was a mouth
with an uncompromising set to it.

As she tried to move she was aware that her head was
being supported by something firm and warm. Putting out
a tentative hand, she found it up against the man's inner
thigh.

She removed it quickly. He was kneeling beside her with
his legs bent beneath him and her head was resting on the
top of his thigh.

As her glance swivelled sideways Jemima saw Bill tow-
ering above her anxiously, and she shuddered. It was his
voice that had brought it all back.

'It's all right, Jemima,' he said awkwardly. 'You had a
little faint—didn't she, Doc?'

'It would appear so,' the stranger said unsmilingly. 'Are
you subject to this kind of thing?'

His voice was brisk but with the familiar soft Cornish drawl and she thought that, whoever he was, this was his land as much as it was hers.

She was raising herself into a sitting position and he put a helping hand beneath her elbow.

'No. I'm not subject to faints,' she said, avoiding his eyes. 'I'd say that it was more of a panic attack than a faint.'

Her father's old friend sighed.

'Seeing the Severn brought it all back, did it, lassie?'

Jemima was on her feet now, holding onto the rail that Jack Trelawney had vaulted to get to her.

'Just a bit,' she admitted, acutely aware of the other man's scrutiny. 'Shall we say, I was unprepared?'

It wasn't strictly true. She could have turned back when she saw that the doors of the lifeboat house were open, but she hadn't, had she?

Maybe subconsciously she'd wanted to get to grips with her fears and phobias in those first few moments of arrival. Whatever the reason, she'd discovered one thing. She wasn't over it. Perhaps she never would be.

'I'll be all right now,' she told the stranger with hair as gold as the summer sun. 'My car is parked down the side street there…and I *am* a doctor.'

'Hmm,' he murmured, as if in no mood for small talk. 'Nevertheless, I don't think you should drive. I'll take you to where you're going.'

Jemima could feel her colour rising. She didn't want to arrive at Surf Cottage with this intimidating stranger. On this brief visit to her native habitat she'd wanted to appear cool, calm, and in control. Not have to endure being dropped off as some sort of wilting parcel who'd had the vapours at the sight of the local lifeboat.

'Do you know Surf Cottage?' she asked politely, as he

switched on the engine of a four-wheel-drive that looked powerful enough to take them to the moon if she'd so requested.

'Yes,' he said briefly.

Deciding that chit-chat was definitely not this man's forte, she leant back against the seat and left it to him to take her to the place that had been her home for twenty-eight years. Until on a never-to-be forgotten night the mainstay had been taken from it.

Her mother's attitude at the time of the tragedy had been complex to say the least. A Londoner, who had never really fitted into the life of the local community of Rockhaven, she had first of all blamed her husband's dedication to the lifeboat service and then had turned on her daughter, accusing Jemima of not trying to save him.

If that had been the extent of her fixations, the young GP who had been the only one available to answer the call for a doctor to go on board on that disastrous night might have been able to cope with Hazel Penrose's bizarre behaviour, but Jemima had been fighting her own feelings of devastation and it hadn't helped when she'd discovered that her mother had been spending all her free time drinking in local bars with hippies, pseudo artists, and beachcombers.

In the end, unable to bear the constant reminders of how her father had met his death, and weary of finding the house constantly filled with her mother's new friends, Jemima had packed her bags and gone to work as a registrar in a hospital in Bristol.

That was how she intended it to stay. This visit to the place that she'd always loved was just that...a visit.

A phone call a couple of weeks ago had brought her mother's voice into her ear, and as Jemima had listened to what she'd had to say her throat had closed up.

'I'm getting married again,' Hazel said, adding before

Jemima could speak, 'It's what your father would expect. He wouldn't want me to be lonely. I'm leading a quieter life now, Jemima, and feel that I'm ready to be a good wife to the man I'm going to marry.'

'And who might that be?' she asked through dry lips. 'Is it anyone I know?'

Her mother laughed and there was relief in it. She'd been expecting some degree of censure from her only daughter and Jemima's calm acceptance of the news was better than she'd hoped for.

'No, you don't know him,' Hazel said. 'James is living temporarily in Rockhaven with his son, but we both want to move away. We've been house-hunting in London. I've always wanted to go back there, as you know. So if you want Surf Cottage, you can have it.'

'I don't think so,' Jemima responded, white-faced at her mother's casual offer. 'There are too many bad memories. Like what happened to Dad and...'

Her voice trailed off and her mother finished the sentence for her. 'What I was like at the time? Well, I've told you, I'm over all that. It was a sort of madness and you were no comfort to me.'

Jemima swallowed hard. Maybe her mother was right. But who had there been to comfort herself? No one! She'd existed from day to day in a grieving limbo, doing what she had to do as a GP at the local surgery and then going home each evening to her mother's rantings and excesses.

It had been the blackest time of her life and even now, two years on, she was still hurting. What had happened earlier was proof of that.

'I haven't seen you before,' Jemima said to the man in the driving seat when she felt that the silence had gone on long enough. 'Are you local?'

He didn't take his eyes off the road as he answered.

'Yes. I haven't always been, but I am now.'

And what was that supposed to mean? she wondered. She could believe that he wasn't originally from Rockhaven. She would have remembered him if he had been. He was the kind of man that a woman wouldn't easily forget.

Broad-shouldered, yet with trim flanks, tanned skin...and the hair! Thick and golden, it curled tightly over his head in a neat short style that made him look like a character from Greek mythology. But the myth ended there, she thought.

This fellow had his feet firmly on the ground. She could tell it from his manner. He drove with cool competence, spoke rarely and, of all things, was in the same profession as herself.

'I'm Jemima Penrose,' she said in another attempt to break the ice.

'Yes. I know.'

'How?'

'Old Bill told me.'

'Oh, yes, of course,' she murmured. 'He was a friend of my father's. I've known him all my life.'

He nodded and she went on. 'Bill spoke as if you were a doctor. Is that so?'

'Yes. I'm a partner in the practice up on Cliff Terrace.'

Hazel's eyes in a pale face widened as she exclaimed, 'Really? I used to work there.'

'So I believe,' he replied, and then the stilted conversation dwindled to a standstill as Surf Cottage came into view.

Perched on the clifftop with its rose-washed walls and mullioned windows, it was just as beautiful as she remembered...from the outside. But what would it be like when she went through the door? Without her father's robust presence it would never be the same.

As the man at her side pulled up on the drive, Jemima brought her mind back to the moment. 'Thanks for everything,' she said quietly. 'For looking after me during a bad moment…and for bringing me home.'

As she opened the car door he smiled for the first time. 'Maybe it's time I introduced myself,' he said in a voice less crisp than previously. 'Does the name Jack Trelawney ring a bell?'

Jemima observed him with puzzled eyes.

'Er, no. Should it?'

'Yes. I would say so. We are shortly to be related. Your mother is going to marry my father. So you'd better watch your step, Jemima Penrose. Big brother will be watching you.'

She blinked, surprise washing over her at the unexpected revelation. And although he was still smiling, had it been some sort of warning he'd just handed out?

There was no time to reply. The bride-to-be and a smaller, older, version of the man called Jack Trelawney had come out onto the porch, and it was clear from their expressions when she got out of the car that they hadn't been expecting her to arrive in such company.

'So, how does this come about?' Hazel Penrose asked, hugging her only child to her. 'Where did you find my daughter, Jack?'

Jemima was waiting for him to say that she'd collapsed and he'd attended her, but to her surprise he said casually, 'We bumped into each other on the seafront and Bill Stennet introduced us.'

Already with something else on her mind, Hazel took the hand of the man beside her and said softly, 'Jemima, this is James Trelawney, Jack's father, the man I'm going to marry.'

'Nice to meet you, Jemima,' he said with a firm hand-shake and a friendly smile, and she thought that the older member of the Trelawneys was the mellower of the two.

It was almost as if his son had already judged her and found her wanting, and if that was the case she would very much like to know why.

'Aren't you going to stay for afternoon tea, Jack?' her mother was asking of the man who had leapt into Jemima's life a short time ago and was now about to get back into his car and depart.

'Can't I'm afraid, Hazel,' he told her. 'I've got afternoon surgery to deal with.'

Her mother pouted and, not to be thwarted, suggested, 'Dinner, then?'

He hesitated, giving Jemima a quick sideways glance, and she wondered if she was the reason for his reluctance to take up the invitation.

'Yes, why not?' Jack said. 'Sevenish?'

'That will be fine,' Hazel cooed.

With a feeling that her new stepbrother-to-be was on better terms with her mother than she was, Jemima watched him stride out of the house. Seconds later, with an inexplicable feeling of relief, she heard him drive off.

When he'd gone Jemima went to stand by the window. It was open and as she breathed in the air it was like sweet wine. There were gulls circling around the headland, and out at sea she caught a glimpse of the bright prow of the lifeboat as it ploughed through the waves on its short trip out.

This time she could watch it calmly. Those moments on the seafront had been in the form of a painful acceptance, a return to reality. Maybe the next time she was close to the Severn it would be all right.

'So, are you going to accept my offer?' her mother was asking from the other side of the room, and Jemima thought that anyone else would have wanted to know how she was. Had she had a good journey? Would she like some refreshment? But not Hazel.

'I've put the kettle on,' the bridegroom-to-be said from the kitchen doorway, and as he smiled across at her Jemima thought that for the next week she was going to be part of a strange foursome.

She'd taken an immediate liking to Jack Trelawney's father and hoped that he knew what he was taking on by marrying her mother.

At first meeting his son had seemed to be a different kettle of fish. Taciturn, extremely confident and critical— if that was the right word to describe his manner towards herself.

Yet it couldn't be. They'd only just met. He knew nothing about her…except what he might have heard from her mother. But surely Hazel wouldn't have discussed her with strangers?

Though the Trelawneys didn't come into that category, did they? They were going to be family and, having met them both, there was only one of them that she could envisage feeling at ease with.

When James had announced that the kettle was on, her mother had got to her feet and disappeared into the kitchen. As she busied herself, making tea, he said, 'I hope you approve of your mother and I getting married, Jemima. She was very unhappy when we first met, but all that's in the past.'

Jemima felt tears prick. Her dad would have liked this friendly man who was going to marry her mother. At least

Hazel had done something right. She'd found herself someone who appeared to be kind and considerate. It was to be
hoped that she would treat James in a similar manner.

'Yes, I do approve,' she said quietly. 'You will be good
for my mother, James, and I hope that she'll be the right
one for you.'

There was a twinkle in the blue eyes that were a paler
version of his son's.

'She's told me all about the past, and that's what it is as
far as I'm concerned…past. We have all got to look to the
future, yourself included.'

On the point of telling him that ever since the loss of
her father she'd lived one day at a time, Jemima was denied
the opportunity as her mother was calling that tea was ready
and would James carry it in.

'You haven't answered my question,' Hazel said as they
ate fruit cake and drank tea from fine china cups.

Jemima looked around her. Surf Cottage was as beautiful
as ever. It was amazing that her mother hadn't changed it,
but for some reason she hadn't and now here her daughter
was, not back five minutes and already under its spell.

'If I were to take you up on your offer, what would I do
for a living?' Jemima said. 'I have to eat.'

'Go back to the practice,' her mother said, as if that were
simple. 'I've invited Helen Granger round to dinner tonight.
There's a vacancy. Tom is leaving. He's going to become
a partner at a practice in Truro.'

'Really! What's brought that about?' Jemima said in surprise.

The man in question had been another reason why she'd
left Rockhaven. He'd professed to be in love with her, had
asked her to marry him, and when she'd refused had turned
nasty. But as she'd never given him any encouragement

Jemima had felt that she hadn't been to blame if Tom Trask had been upset.

'So who is there at the surgery now?' she asked.

'Well, Helen is still practice manager,' her mother replied. 'I can't see her being enticed away by anyone. She loves the place too much. Jack, who you met earlier, is senior partner. He took over from Clive Bradley who retired last summer, and he's now running the place with Bethany Griffiths and Tom to assist—until he goes at the end of the month.'

'I don't think I want to go back,' Jemima said slowly.

Surf Cottage was pulling at her heartstrings but the thought of working with the abrupt stranger she would soon be related to didn't appeal.

Hazel sighed.

'You always were difficult, Jemima. If it had been your dad suggesting it, you wouldn't be quibbling. Surely you see the benefits? I'm offering to give you this place and there might be a job going at the practice. What more could you ask for? James and I have found somewhere to rent in a fashionable part of London and once the wedding is over we'll be off.'

Jemima eyed her sombrely. Her mother had asked what more she could ask for. Hazel would have little patience with her were she to enlighten her as to what she *would* like to ask for.

She yearned for this place to be as it was. Free of painful memories. For her father to come striding through the door with fresh fish on a hook and the tang of the sea on him. To be able to sleep the night through without the tortured dreams that plagued her.

It was strange though. If it had been anyone else but Hazel she might have thought there had been a note of pleading in her voice, but that wasn't her way. Yet

Jemima's eyes widened when her mother went on to say, 'I'd feel happier if you were back home, instead of being stuck in Bristol all on your own.'

'I'm not on my own,' she protested. 'I have friends at the hospital and I'm dating one of the admin staff there.'

Her mother ignored the protest and, picking up the tray with the tea-things on it, she looked down at her daughter's dark head.

'Yes, well, let's see what Helen has to say, eh?'

'Hazel is very keen for you to come back to Rockhaven,' James said with a sympathetic smile when she'd gone into the kitchen.

'I don't see why.'

'Maybe she wants to make amends. I know that you both had a very difficult time when your father died. You in particular, Jemima.'

She nodded. 'I can't deny that.'

He got to his feet. 'Let's take your cases upstairs, shall we?'

'Yes, why not? But first I need to know which room I'm in.'

Hazel was bridling in the doorway behind them.

'In your own, of course!' she snapped.

Jemima had unpacked. She'd touched every single item in her room with loving hands, then had showered and changed, and now she was standing on the headland with Surf Cottage behind her and the capricious Atlantic in front.

She wasn't looking forward to tonight's little dinner party one bit, she decided as the breeze from the sea lifted the long swathe of her hair.

Helen Granger, the middle-aged practice manager and mother of teenage twin boys, had been one of the few people who hadn't criticised her for leaving Rockhaven, and

Jemima knew she wouldn't attempt to persuade her to do anything against her will.

It was the other person who was going to be present that was making her nervous. It was only hours since they'd first met and then it had only been briefly. But since finding herself resting against his leg on the seafront, she'd discovered that Jack Trelawney would be well and truly in her life if she came back to Rockhaven. Not only as a colleague, but as a relation.

And what was it he'd said? That 'big brother' would be watching her. Why, for heaven's sake?

When Jack pulled up in front of the house that evening, the first thing he saw was the slender figure on the nearby headland, etched against the glowing orange of a setting autumn sun.

She was very still, wrapped in remoteness, and he wondered how she was reacting to the news that they would soon be stepbrother and -sister.

He supposed it was all a bit much, coming back to Rockhaven, having the fainting episode on the seafront…and then finding out who he was.

His name hadn't rang a bell so obviously Hazel hadn't told her daughter much about him, which was strange as he hadn't noticed any clam-like tendencies about the woman his father was going to marry.

She'd certainly kept nothing back about her daughter. When they'd first been introduced Hazel had gone into great detail about how Jemima had gone to do her own thing and had left her mother griefstricken and friendless.

Tom hadn't been exactly reticent about her either. There'd been a few comments about how she'd led him on and then dumped him, and all in all Jack hadn't exactly been looking forward to the return of the prodigal daughter.

When he'd taken hold of her as she'd stood swaying on the seafront he'd had no idea who she was, but Bill had soon put him in the picture and ever since he'd been trying to adjust the impression he'd had in his mind of her to the actual person. On the face of it they seemed very different.

'Admiring the sunset?' a voice asked from behind Jemima, and she turned to find her golden-haired acquaintance of the afternoon observing her.

Her cheeks were wet with the tears that memories had brought forth and she didn't want this man to see them. Yet neither did she want to brush them away as if ashamed of her emotions.

'Yes. I am. Watching the sun go down from this spot is one of the things I've missed most while I've been away.'

'So why did you go?'

'I beg your pardon?'

'I'm sorry. But one only needs to look at you to see that you belong here.'

It was true. There was something about Jemima that made him think of a sea nymph. In a pale green silk dress that the wind was flattening against her fine-boned slenderness, the pale waif of the seafront had gone and in her place was a beautiful Cornish maid with tear-damp cheeks.

But he was letting himself be influenced by outward appearances, he told himself. A few tears and a degree of feminine allure weren't going to wipe out all his preconceived ideas about her. There was many a canker inside a beautiful shell.

Unaware of the jumble of his thoughts, Jemima gave a wry smile.

'I did fit in here…once. But life doesn't stand still, does it? Unfortunately.'

'It would be very boring if it did,' he told her, and saw her shiver.

'Was it something I said?' he asked. 'Or is the wind getting cooler?'

She wrapped her arms around her. 'It's October and it does chill off at this time of night. Shall we go inside?'

They found Helen seated by the fire with a glass of sherry in her hand when they went inside and Hazel and James bustling around in the kitchen.

'Helen! How lovely to see you,' Jemima said with a break in her voice as the greying practice manager smiled across at them.

It was the first time he'd seen Jemima show any emotion, Jack thought as he deposited himself in the nearest chair. She'd been limp and unresisting when he'd cradled her to him earlier, and out there on the headland her remoteness had persisted, although to be fair he'd thought that she'd been shedding a tear when he'd broken into her reverie.

'Are you going to come back to us?' Helen said as Jemima perched down beside her. 'You know that Tom's going... I thought that might make you think about coming back into general practice—ours for choice.'

Jemima's face was shadowed in the fire's flickering light. Everything was moving too fast. It was her first day back and already the cocoon that she'd wrapped around herself ever since leaving Rockhaven was being pulled apart.

This was meant to be a visit...and only that...but already the past was reaching out to her and the present unfolding in a way that she didn't think she wanted it to.

Did she want to come back here? And, more important still, did the man with the cool blue eyes who was sitting opposite her want to be in close contact with her both at work and within his family?

Obviously he'd joined the practice after she'd left so he would have no idea whether she was good at the job or not, but it was clear that he was dubious about her for some reason.

And with regard to the vacancy that her rejected suitor was creating, surely Jack would have the last word when it came to that. He seemed to be on reasonably good terms with her mother, but was giving no indication that he was looking forward to furthering his acquaintance with herself.

'I don't think so,' Jemima said at last, adding with a quick glance at Jack's silent figure, 'Everyone at the practice mightn't feel the same about me as you do, Helen.'

The older woman laughed.

'If you're referring to the senior partner, let's ask him. Jack will soon tell you if he's not in favour of my suggestion.' She gave an affectionate glance in his direction, 'Won't you, Dr Trelawney?'

Jack uncrossed long legs and eyed them both thoughtfully.

'You can rest assured on that,' he told her, and whatever else he might have had to say had to be put on hold as Hazel was asking them to take their seats in the dining room as the meal was about to be served.

CHAPTER TWO

THERE was no further mention of Jemima rejoining the practice during the meal, and she wondered if Jack was trying to think of an excuse for not going along with the idea.

Why was it that she never seemed to get it right in her dealings with the opposite sex? she asked herself. Were they conscious that she was wary...loth to get involved?

In recent years there'd been the embarrassing one-sided thing with Tom that she hadn't come out of very well, in spite of being completely blameless. Then the lukewarm affair with Mark Emmerson which had ended with a nasty taste in the mouth. She always seemed to be the 'hunted', rather than the 'hunter', but maybe she'd only herself to blame.

Though there had once been a time, long ago, when she hadn't minded being singled out. In her last year at medical school. Gabe Torrance, one of the lecturers, had made a play for her and she'd fallen madly in love.

A laconic, attractive American, he had been on a six-month exchange with an English professor and had relished every moment of the adoration of the inexperienced young student.

But while her love had still been in its first blooming, his time had come to go back, and he'd gone with scarcely a backward glance, leaving her with such a feeling of loss that she'd thought she'd never get over it.

She had, of course, but the memory was always there and, when it was followed by the much greater loss of her

father and the alienation from her mother, she had decided
that henceforth she would tread warily when it came to
giving her affections.

But this was a different matter. She'd only met this
golden-haired Cornishman today, and reason told her that
he wasn't the kind of man who would need an excuse not
to hire her. His type came straight out with what they had
to say and usually didn't beat about the bush.

If he did have cause for being wary of her, she may as
well forget the whole thing, which was a laugh as only
minutes ago there hadn't been anything she'd fancied doing
less than going back to the practice just down the road.

For some reason her mother had stopped harping about
it and Helen hadn't pursued her laughing challenge to the
man sitting opposite, so was she disappointed that the subject had been dropped?

No, she wasn't. She was allowing herself to be tempted
into doing something that had been the last thing in her
mind when she'd agreed to come back for her mother's
wedding.

It was the house that was doing it, of course. The sight,
shape and sounds of Surf Cottage were making her want
to stay. But if going back to the practice where Jack now
ruled the roost was going to be part of the deal, wouldn't
she be better off finding another niche where a doctor was
needed? Or, if that wasn't possible, she could always work
in a seafront café or, as a last resort, take tourists for trips
along the coast.

But that would involve the sea, the vicious enemy that
had taken her father away. Could she cope with coming
face to face with it again?

Lifeboat men had been lost before along the coast where
she'd been brought up. It was a dangerous occupation. Yet

there were always those ready to take the place of a man
who'd perished.

She'd known about the dangers, lived with the knowledge all her life, but never had she expected to be a helpless, horrified spectator when the sea had taken her father.

She'd been on board because she'd been the GP on call
when the message had come through that a fishing smack
had been in trouble in the storm that had been rattling
around Rockhaven.

A crew member had been badly injured and they'd asked
for a doctor to accompany the lifeboat crew. So, as she had
done on other occasions, Jemima had gone out with her
father and the other men, and until he'd loosened his life-
line for a second to get to the wheelhouse more quickly at
the height of the storm he'd been in control.

Numb with the knowledge that her father was either dead
or drowning somewhere in the raging sea, Jemima went on
board the other vessel after they'd managed to attach a tow
rope and treated the injured man.

In the end the crew of the fishing boat and their vessel
were brought to safety by the lifeboat. Stephen Penrose had
been the only casualty and when they eventually reached
dry land after a frantic search of the storm-tossed ocean,
Jemima stumbled ashore dazed with grief.

Her father's body was washed up further along the coast
two days later and the nightmare that had started on the
night of the storm continued.

When the meal was over Jemima offered to clear away and
once it was done it was a relief to be in the kitchen, washing up, away from Jack's watchful gaze.

The conversation during dinner had been casual and
friendly but Jemima had felt there had been undertones to

it. And if Hazel had noticed that her daughter had had very little to contribute, for once she'd let it pass.

It was clear that Helen and Jack got on well, and Hazel and James seemed content enough with their guests and each other. She was the odd one out, Jemima thought. A familiar feeling of late. Could she endure a week of this? A week of putting on an act? Pretending that she was happy to be there when it hurt all the time?

'I'll wipe if you'll find me a cloth,' Jack said from behind Jemima, and she decided that his habit of suddenly appearing from the rear was extremely offputting.

'In the drawer beside you,' she told him, and as he planted himself alongside her she threw caution to the winds and let him see that she was reading his mind.

'I'm sorry that Helen put you on the spot earlier,' she said smoothly. 'It wasn't my idea that I come back to work in the practice. I have every intention of going back to Bristol once the wedding is over.'

'So your mother's offer to give you this place isn't acceptable,' he said with a quick sideways look at her set face.

'If you mean, would I like to live in Surf Cottage—of course I would. I adore the place. I was brought up here. But everything has changed. Me most of all.'

'So you haven't come back on the off chance that you might get your hands on your old home?'

With her hands deep in the soap suds she turned to face him, anger kindling inside her.

'Get my hands on! You have a strange turn of phrase. It is…or was…my home. I have a right to be here if I want. Just as I have a right to apply for the vacancy at the practice. Although I can see that it would be a waste of time, as for some reason you're very critical of me. But you don't need to worry, Dr Trelawney. I won't be doing that. I'm not in the habit of pushing myself where I'm not wanted.'

'Maybe not,' he remarked calmly, 'but there's one thing you are guilty of.'

'And what's that?'

'Jumping to conclusions. I don't recollect saying that I would object to you applying for the vacancy that has arisen because of your ex-boyfriend leaving the practice. You say that you have the right to apply and, of course, you have. No one can stop you.'

Jemima managed to refrain from informing him that Tom Trask was not her ex-boyfriend. That she wouldn't fancy him if he were the last man on earth. Instead, she commented drily, 'And no one can stop *you* from turning me down.'

'Oh, yes, they can. It has to be a joint decision between Bethany Griffiths and myself. So, you see, I don't rule the roost entirely.'

'Surprise! Surprise!'

'If you could put the sarcasm to one side for a moment, might I point out that your first decision has to be whether you want to come back here to live? If you don't, the job situation doesn't arise.'

Jemima sighed.

'I wasn't expecting any of this. It was just a visit to be present at my mother's wedding, and look what it's snowballing into.'

'If you don't want to come back, I don't think any of us will be surprised. After all, you were quick enough to depart,' he said levelly.

'How dare you judge me?' she flared. 'You weren't even around.'

'True,' he agreed calmly, 'but I've been ''around'' watching my father help your mother pick up the pieces.'

Jemima began to dry her hands.

'I've had enough of this,' she told him tersely. 'We haven't known each other twenty-four hours and you're preaching the gospel according to Jack Trelawney. I hope that your behaviour will be whiter than white when something happens to *your* father, but unless James is contemplating bigamy, you won't have your mother to cope with like I did.'

And without giving him time to find an answer to that she whizzed past him back into the sitting room where Helen eyed her red cheeks questioningly.

'So, have you and Jack sorted anything out?' she asked.

'Yes,' Jemima told her through tight lips. 'He's quite happy for me to apply.'

As Helen nodded approvingly, her glance went to the man framed in the doorway behind Jemima with an expression on his face that was giving nothing away.

'And are you going to do so?' the practice manager persisted.

'Why not?' Jemima said with reckless perversity. 'I've nothing to lose. My mother has offered me the house. So all I need now is a job.'

And the chances of the senior partner offering it to me are extremely remote, she thought grimly. So in the end there will be no decisions to make.

'Why don't you call into the surgery for a chat one day,' Helen suggested as she was leaving. 'The rest of the staff are the same. Jack is the only newcomer.'

Jemima managed a smile. She liked Helen and it was hard to refuse her anything.

'I'll think about it. What would be the best time? Or, more to the point, when is Tom not likely to be there?'

'Late morning. He'll be out on his calls.'

'I'll bear that in mind if I decide to come,' she told her.

Jack was getting ready to leave but first he reminded his father, 'Dad, don't forget we're having a fitting at the tailor's tomorrow.'

James nodded. 'I'm not likely to forget that, am I? And if I did, Hazel would soon be reminding me.'

'I'll show you my outfit when the men have gone,' Hazel said to her daughter, 'and you can show me yours. I want my bridesmaid to do me justice.'

Jemima was goggling at her.

'Bridesmaid! You never said.'

'I would have though it was obvious. You're the only female relation I've got…and my daughter.'

'You might have told me. Supposing I haven't brought anything suitable.'

'Then we'll go out and buy something.'

James had been smiling his placating smile while the discourse had been taking place, but his son's face had tightened and Jemima thought, Here we go again. He's obviously of the same opinion as my mother…that I'm determined to be difficult.

Driving back to his flat over an art gallery by the harbour, Jack was in thoughtful mood. It had been a strange day. The prospective stepsister he'd been reluctant to meet had turned out to be a total surprise.

From what he'd heard of her previously, he'd expected Jemima Penrose to be hard and manipulative, but instead she'd been…what? A mixture of many things?

In the first moments of their meeting she'd been limp and helpless at his feet. Then out on the headland in the setting sun she'd seemed mysterious and alluring. But later, in the kitchen, with a big cotton apron over the lovely silk dress, he'd discovered that there was fire in her, too. That she wasn't prepared to let him criticise her without a protest. He couldn't blame her for that. He'd had no right to say what he had.

Then there'd been the bridesmaid confusion. It was typical of Hazel to put the blame on someone else when she'd taken something for granted, and fleetingly he'd been on Jemima's side.

He was fond of his future stepmother but knew her limitations, and one of them was expecting everyone to fall in with her wishes, whether they wanted to or not.

It was clear that Jemima had been closer to her father, and anyone could understand her anguish at being present when he'd died. But it had been Hazel who'd been left without a husband, and when her daughter had packed her bags and left she'd had no one, and in spite of her frivolous exterior, he didn't doubt that she'd grieved for her husband as much as anyone.

Would the Jekyll-and-Hyde creature that was Jemima Penrose apply for the vacancy at the practice? he wondered. Or had it been merely bravado that had made her tell Helen that she was going to? And if she did, how would he feel about it?

He didn't know, and indecision was something foreign to him. Normally clear-thinking and objective, for once he wasn't sure. But maybe there wouldn't be a problem. He'd like to bet that she would go back to Bristol. If that happened, they would only meet up on the rare family occasion.

So why didn't he feel relieved?

Jack wasn't the only one who was going over the day's happenings. As Jemima lay in the room that hadn't known her presence for two long years, she was relieved to be off the roller-coaster of events that she'd found herself on from the moment of her return to Rockhaven.

They'd been dangling carrots in front of her, her mother and Helen. First the offer of the house from Hazel and then Helen's suggestion that she return to the practice.

It was a strange feeling, as no one had exactly begged her to stay when she'd said she was leaving. But now they were at her from all sides to come back. Everyone except Jack Trelawney who, it would seem, saw her as a bad risk from every angle.

With the sound of the sea in her ears as it lapped against the shingle on the beach below, she drifted off to sleep at last and for once there were no nightmares.

A fact that she was immediately conscious of when she awoke the next morning. Was it because she was back home? she wondered. Or because she'd seen the lifeboat in reality once more and laid its ghost to rest? Whatever it was, she didn't feel as frazzled as she had yesterday.

James had left much later than his son the previous night, so there would be only Helen and herself for breakfast— and unless her mother had changed a great deal, she wouldn't be surfacing for a long time yet.

Jemima saw that the tide was some way out and all was calm. For the moment the lion was tamed. There were no huge breakers bounding in to crash against the rocks below. With a sudden longing to feel the fine gold sand beneath her feet, she went out into the chilly October morning.

She could see two people swimming in the distance as she walked along the beach, and when she turned to retrace her steps they'd left the water and were walking towards her.

Her step faltered. There was no mistaking that physique and the damp golden locks. The bigger of the two was Jack Trelawney out for an early swim. And his companion?

Obviously female if jutting breasts in a bikini top were

anything to go by. Yet she was petite, and with a mop of dark hair lying flatly against her head.

He'd seen her. Was waiting for her to draw level. Unable to help herself, Jemima's eyes were drawn to the lithe, tanned body that was covered in droplets of sea water.

'You're up early, Jemima,' he said in brief greeting.

'Yes. I couldn't wait to get down to the beach,' she told him, and immediately wished she hadn't. It was letting him see how much it all meant to her.

'I can imagine,' he said, and she knew he'd guessed her thoughts. He turned to his companion who was beginning to shiver in the cool wind. 'Can I introduce a neighbour of mine? Emma Carson.'

He was wrapping a large beach towel around the dark-haired woman's shoulders as he spoke and something about the gesture made Jemima wonder whether he was merely concerned that his companion was getting cold or if there was a deeper meaning to his action.

'Emma, this is Jemima Penrose, soon to become my step-sister,' he said quickly, as if he'd already decided that they had better be on their way.

The other woman extended a cold, wet hand and as Jemima shook it she looked into a pair of dark eyes that were full of startled surprise.

'You never said!' she exclaimed, turning to her companion.

Jemima couldn't resist putting her oar in.

'It's a case of the return of the reluctant bridesmaid, I'm afraid.'

'I'm not with you,' Emma said.

Somebody else was, though, and, taking his companion's arm, he said evenly, 'Point taken. Now, if you'll excuse us, we'll be off before we freeze to death.'

So much for endearing yourself to Jack Trelawney,

Jemima thought as she climbed back up to the cottage. She was as bad as he was. They were going to have to learn to get on with each other, having been thrown into a relationship that neither of them seemed to want.

They owed it to their parents to be pleasant. After all, they were both adults and should be capable of behaving reasonably.

Hazel had looked over the outfit that Jemima had brought for the wedding and had announced it suitable for her daughter to wear as bridesmaid.

Fortunately the smart fine wool suit of lilac, with a darker mauve hat and shoes, didn't clash with Hazel's outfit of cream silk, so another awkward situation was averted.

The ceremony was to take place at three o'clock on the Saturday in the biggest church in the area. A choice that had filled Jemima with relief.

If it had been in the tiny church on the seafront where traditionally seamen and their families had always worshipped, she didn't think she could have coped.

But for once Hazel was being tactful, or else she'd decided that it wasn't posh enough. Whatever the reason Jemima was grateful.

It was Wednesday and Jemima still hadn't been to see the people at the practice. She was spending the days wandering along the seafront, browsing in the shops and eyeing the ever-present ocean with wary eyes.

But all the time at the back of her mind Jemima was conscious that before she said a word to anyone she had to decide if she wanted to come back home.

It was that one word that was bemusing her. Home. Rockhaven *was* her home. She'd let circumstances drive her away from it and now they were combining to bring her back. But did she want to let them?

Maybe the answer lay at the surgery. She hadn't seen anything of Jack Trelawney since that meeting on the beach with his attractive neighbour. Perhaps another foray into what had started off as a rather fraught relationship was called for…and then she would decide whether to apply for the vacancy.

Jemima found herself smiling at her optimism. There was nothing to say that she would get the job if she did. There could be lots of other folk after it.

Go and see them…him, she told herself, and play it from there. He won't bite you!

As Helen had suggested, she left it until late morning before presenting herself at the old stone building where she had worked with zest and contentment until her father's death. But the strategy didn't pay off. As Jemima was about to enter, the door opened and Tom came striding out.

In that first dismayed glance she saw that he hadn't changed. Sandy brows beneath a thinning mop of the same colour were scowling at her and the mouth from which he had hissed his disappointment at her was still the thin line that she remembered.

'So it *is* true!' he said. 'You *are* after your old job.'

'I'm not after anything,' she told him coolly. 'Except a word with my old friends.'

'And I suppose I don't come into that category.'

'You might have done if you hadn't been so hateful when I wouldn't marry you.'

He ignored that.

'I take it you've heard I'm leaving?'

'Yes. I've heard. I believe you're going to Truro.'

'Correct. I've had enough of this place. Thought you had, too.'

'So did I,' she said wryly. She wasn't going to explain that now she was home she was having second thoughts. Knowing him, he might just decide to stay to spite her.

But it seemed that he was set on going as his next remark was, 'I'll be senior partner at the new place, which is something I've wanted for a long time. It should have been me here, but I didn't stand a chance when Trelawney came along. You're welcome to him if you're thinking of taking my place.'

On that cryptic note he pushed past her as if he'd wasted enough time already.

'So much for Mr Sunshine,' a voice said from nearby, and Jemima looked up to see Bethany approaching.

As the two women shook hands Jemima felt as if some of Tom's acidity had been banished. A gentle, extremely competent forty-year-old, Bethany was the last person she would have any concerns about were she to come back, Jemima thought. They'd always got on well, though the other woman had never taken a call-out on the lifeboat. Tom had once, and he'd never stopped moaning about it afterwards as he'd been seasick all the time he'd been on board.

So in the past, before that dreadful night, it had been Jemima who'd gone when a doctor had been needed. Who had filled the gap she'd left, she didn't know, and for the last two years she hadn't cared.

If she were to come back it would have to be understood that she couldn't do it again. Not for anything or anyone. The recollection came back of Jack's presence beside the craft on that day when she'd surfaced to find herself supported against him.

Had he been there because he'd taken over as the crew's

medical officer on call? She wouldn't be surprised. That one wouldn't bat an eyelid in a force ten gale. She could bet on it.

'So you've come to see us at last,' Bethany was saying. 'I was beginning to think you'd be going back to Bristol without popping in.'

Jemima shook her head.

'I've been trying to pluck up courage ever since I saw Helen on my first day back.'

'And now here you are. Come inside and we'll have a coffee to take away the taste of Tom's tantrums.'

'You know, we never replaced you,' Bethany said when they'd seated themselves in her consulting room. 'We've used trainees, locums and the rest to fill the gap. So there would be a vacancy even if Tom wasn't leaving.'

'I wouldn't want to come back if he was still here,' Jemima told her.

'No. I suppose not. That one has done his best to blacken your name to anyone who would listen, though we both know that it's a case of hell having no fury like a would-be lover scorned.'

'Exactly,' Jemima agreed. 'But there's Jack Trelawney, too. I haven't exactly hit it off with him either. You know that his father is to marry my mother so, whether I like it or not, we're going to be thrown together from a family point of view, and as for working with him…'

'That would depend on how well you acquitted yourself,' his voice said from the doorway. 'There's no time for personalities in a busy general practice.'

As Jemima swung round to face him she was thinking that he actually sounded as if he was expecting her to come back, and was telling her that anything other than the job was of no interest to him.

Maybe she could cope with that. But could she cope with

seeing the Severn go out into rough seas, and her father's lobster pots empty and unattended? Yet deep down she knew it was what he would want for her…that she be home, instead of hiding away in Bristol.

It had been her mother's bizarre behaviour that had driven her away in the first place and, strangely, it had been her mother who had been instrumental in bringing her back to Rockhaven.

'So you'd be willing to take a chance on me, then?' she said coolly.

'I'd take a chance on anyone if they were a good doctor,' he replied levelly, 'and if you've come to say that you want to join us, maybe the three of us had better have a chat.'

Jemima felt her knees go weak and this time it was nothing to do with the lifeboat. Now was the moment to tell him that she hadn't come to do anything of the kind, but the words wouldn't come and she followed him meekly into his consulting room, with Bethany bringing up the rear.

'There are two things I'd like to make clear,' Jemima said firmly a little later when all the finer details of a new contract at the practice had been discussed. 'If the lifeboat gets any calls for a doctor to sail with it, I don't want it to be me. That's the first thing. The other is that it will be a month before I can join you, as they'll be expecting me to work out my notice at Bristol.'

All through the discussion they'd just had Jack hadn't been friendly or unfriendly, just brisk and businesslike, and even though it was galling to be kept at a distance, it was also a relief.

And now that they had more or less agreed all the details of her employment, Jemima had decided that it had been time to let him see that she had some stipulations of her own and, if he wasn't happy about them…too bad.

But it seemed that he saw no problem with what she'd just said and Bethany, who had only made the odd comment during the interview, didn't seem too bothered either.

'*I* take the calls if a doctor is required on the Severn,' he said. 'I've done it ever since I came. Like you, I've been around boats most of my life. The only problem would be if I wasn't available. Then they would have to contact another practice. But as we aren't called out that often, it should work all right.'

Thank goodness he wasn't going to come out with any platitudes such as 'life has to go on' or 'don't you think it's time you pulled yourself together', she thought. From what she'd seen of him so far, it wouldn't have been surprising.

'And with regard to your notice,' he was saying. 'Of course we would expect you to fulfil any commitments in your present post.'

His eye was on the clock and he got to his feet.

'I think that we've covered everything, Jemima, and now, if you'll excuse me, I have patients to attend to.'

Jack held out his hand and as Jemima shook it tentatively she was aware of strong fingers and a tanned wrist encircled by a gold watch.

It was the first time they'd touched and she couldn't believe the effect it was having on her. Her pulses were racing, her blood warming, and all they were doing was shaking hands. What would it feel like to be really held by Jack? she wondered.

There was a look in his eyes that told her he was reading her mind again, and she withdrew her clasp with a feeling that she'd just done something very stupid by deciding to come back to Rockhaven.

Life in Bristol was uneventful, at times almost boring, but it was painless. Coming back here was going to open raw wounds. Her vulnerability would be out in the open, and if this very attractive man was going to be around all the time, what had she let herself in for?

She could tell that he disapproved of her, and if he'd heard her mother's version of past events and Tom's imaginary grievances, she supposed it wasn't surprising. But did she want to walk in the shadow of his censure?

Jemima straightened her shoulders. One thing she did want was to come back to Surf Cottage and Rockhaven. She'd finally got around to admitting it.

For the rest of the day Jack was asking himself what had possessed him to agree to give Jemima her old job back.

He was quite capable of measuring the worth of a person without anyone else's assistance, but what he'd heard of her before her arrival hadn't been good and he'd been prepared to dislike her on sight. On the contrary, she'd been a surprise. Nothing at all like he'd expected. So had it been curiosity that had made him take her back into the practice?

Everyone agreed she was a good doctor and maybe that was where she excelled. Her personal relationships didn't seem to be as successful.

He'd felt her hand tremble when he'd held it in his, and thought that she wasn't as cool as she would like him to think. Unexpectedly, he'd had to admit that he wasn't as averse to her as he'd expected to be.

For one thing, she was quite beautiful in a restrained sort of way—nut-brown hair, hazel eyes and a sort of fine-boned slenderness that brought the sea nymph to mind again.

Forget the woman, he told himself firmly as the old oak door of a small house down a side street near the harbour swung open and he prepared to make his last visit of the day.

'Come in, Doctor,' a worried young mother said when she saw him. 'It's my little girl, Jasmine. She's got a high temperature and is complaining that her ears hurt.'

The child was lying on a couch in the small sitting room and she was very flushed. The burning heat of fever was there when Jack touched her forehead, and when he took her temperature it was soaring.

'She won't eat. Says that it hurts when she tries,' her mother told him anxiously. 'But she won't open her mouth for me to look.'

'You'll open it for me, though, won't you, Jasmine?' he said gently. 'I can't make you better if I don't know where it hurts.'

Big brown eyes in a flushed face were observing him warily, and after a second's silence she slowly opened her mouth.

'Now, say ''ah'' for me,' Jack wheedled in the same gentle tone. When she obliged he whistled softly and, turning to her mother, said, 'There's a lot of inflammation there.'

He felt the young girl's neck.

'There are enlarged lymph nodes in the neck, too. Jasmine has tonsilitis. Put her to bed, give her plenty of fluids, and if she's no better in twenty-four hours, or if you see pus on her tonsils, send for me again.'

When he got outside the sun was about to set over the sea again and his mind went back to Jemima's first day back in Rockhaven, how he'd found her standing motionless on the headland, looking out to sea, and how it hadn't been hard to guess what had been going through her mind.

So far she was a mystery. She wasn't giving anything away regarding her feelings, except for that firm reminder that she wouldn't be going out on the lifeboat ever again.

It took some guts to go out on an emergency at the best

of times. But Jemima's appetite for sailing on the high seas
had gone and he couldn't blame her for that.

But why had she made her loss worse by deserting her
mother at such a time? He would have thought they would
have clung to each other in their grief.

Jack gave a wry smile. He was the last one to be pon-
tificating on the relationships of others, with his track record. A disastrous marriage that had left him very wary of
women in general wasn't anything to boast about, and with
the thought there came to mind a face that he'd hoped never
to see again.

CHAPTER THREE

'SO YOU'VE decided to see sense at last,' Hazel said that night when Jemima told her about the hastily convened interview earlier in the day.

'We're all in favour of you coming back, you know,' she said persuasively. 'Helen, as practice manager, thinks it's a good idea. So does Bethany, and both James and I want to see you settled back here before we move to London.'

Jemima's face had become stiff.

'So it's a case of everybody knowing what's best for me except myself, is it? And what about Jack? Does he think it's a good idea? Or is he doing you all a favour by offering me the job? I have a feeling that he isn't exactly bursting to make my acquaintance.'

Hazel shuffled her feet uncomfortably. 'I want you to come back to Rockhaven because I was responsible for you leaving in the first place. The only excuse I have is that I couldn't cope when I lost your dad and ended up behaving like a crazy woman, thinking only of myself.

'You say that you're happy in Bristol, but I know you, Jemima. I know how much this place means to you, and if I'm willing to give you the cottage, getting your old job back at the practice completes the package.'

'Can you afford it?' Jemima asked doubtfully.

Her mother smiled.

'Yes, of course. I wouldn't be offering if I couldn't. So is that it, then? You're going to take up where you left off?'

'I suppose so.'

It would have made her feel better if she could have told Hazel that nothing would be as it had been before. That this beautiful Cornish paradise was too full of memories. But it would be cruel not to accept the new closeness that her mother was offering.

Hazel's wedding day dawned cold and clear, and as Jemima walked the deserted beach in the early morning there was no damp blond head to be seen above the waves.

What would Jack be doing at this moment? she wondered. Eating his breakfast? Pressing his wedding suit? Preparing to take the short Saturday morning surgery? Or maybe she was looking too far ahead. It was only seven o'clock. How did she know that he wasn't in the process of waking up beside his curvy neighbour?

She didn't. And was she bothered if he was? She knew little about him, apart from the knowledge that he was James's son and the senior partner at the practice.

Where did he live, for instance? She would ask Hazel when she got back. It couldn't be far away, or he wouldn't swim from this beach.

She hadn't slept well. Not because the nightmares had returned, but because she'd wakened in the middle of the night to the realisation of what she'd done. And with that knowledge had come the thought that she was going to be working with the most attractive man she'd ever met, and it meant exactly nothing because to him she was just two things—a prescription pad on two legs and a family encumbrance.

The wedding was at three o'clock and as Jemima followed Hazel down the aisle she was relieved to see only a smattering of local folk seated in the big Anglican church across

from the post office. The last thing she felt like was coping
with a crowd of those who'd known both her parents.

As they'd got ready for the ceremony she'd felt closer
to her mother than she had in years. Their brief chat and
Hazel's unexpected apology, not in keeping with her belief
that she was never in the wrong, were responsible for that,
and it was with a lighter heart that Jemima had gone to the
wedding.

'I don't look old enough to have a daughter your age,
do I?' Hazel had said as she'd admired herself in the cream
brocade suit that was her bridal outfit.

Jemima had hid a smile. Hazel didn't want any compe-
tition, even from her own daughter, yet she didn't have to
worry. Her own outfit was smart and suited her beautifully,
but James would have eyes only for her mother.

And who would his son's unreadable blue gaze be on?
she wondered. Not herself, that was for sure.

But as the two men got to their feet at the sound of the
bridal march and Jack glanced over his shoulder, she found
her assumption to be wrong.

His glance went past her mother and was on herself, and
if she hadn't been so sure that he had doubts about her,
Jemima might have thought that she saw approval there.

Whatever it was, he spoilt it. As they each took a step
back, leaving the bridal pair to make their vows, he said in
a low voice, 'I thought the colours that you're wearing were
for secondary mourning.'

'How do you know I'm not mourning the prospect of
our prospective family alliance?' she replied.

That brought a smile to his face.

'Point taken, little sister,' he said, and at the minister's
request he stepped forward and produced the ring with a
solemnity that belied their whispered exchange of words.

Little sister…big brother, Jemima thought. Not if she could help it!

But the uniting of the two families continued after they'd left the church and were having a meal at Rockhaven's best hotel.

'I'll feel happier knowing that you've got Jack nearby when we're living in London,' her mother said to Jemima after the man in question had toasted them in champagne.

'You'll look after your new stepsister, won't you?' she asked of him.

'Why? Does she need looking after?' he asked calmly, and Jemima thought hotly that they were discussing her as if she wasn't there…again!

'No! She doesn't. She can look after herself!' Jemima snapped.

'Bravo, my dear,' James said, and it occurred to her that it would have been a more suitable match if Hazel had married the son instead of the father. They were two of a kind.

Yet that wasn't fair. Her mum had been both apologetic and generous since her return, and it *was* Hazel's wedding day, so Jemima smiled at Jack and said, 'We need to get to know each other first, don't we?'

'Absolutely,' he agreed with a heartiness that told her he'd read her mind and was prepared to play his part…for the moment.

Hazel and James were driving to London after the meal and Jemima intended returning to Bristol the following day. It would be four long weeks before she came back, and as she and Jack waved the bridal couple out of sight a little later the feeling of unreality was back.

Surf Cottage was hers. In an act of quixotic generosity her mother had given it to her. Papers were waiting at

Hazel's solicitors for Jemima to sign, and once that was done she would be the legal owner.

Her dad would have liked that if he'd been here. Her mother had never been happy in the house, but she herself loved the place as much as he had, and ever since she'd decided to stay she'd been sure she'd felt his approval.

'So that's that,' the man at her side said as the car disappeared from view.

Jemima nodded.

'Mmm, it is. I hope they'll be happy.'

'They will,' Jack said confidently. 'My father will keep Hazel in check and she'll liven him up. Which leaves you and me on the perimeter so to speak.'

'You won't find me under your feet,' she said quickly. 'Either socially or workwise. Don't feel that you've been landed with the role of watchdog. I am, as I said before, quite capable of taking care of myself.'

'I can well believe it. Anyone who's prepared to sail with the lifeboat is no weakling. For that matter, the same applies to anyone who chooses medicine for a career.'

'So why have you got such a down on me?'

He looked away.

'I haven't.'

'Oh, no? There's doubt and distrust written all over your face every time we meet. It wouldn't be so bad if I knew why.'

'I can't distrust you all that much, or I wouldn't have agreed to take you back into the practice,' he pointed out equably enough, but Jemima could see that he wasn't happy with the way the conversation was going.

'It's our parents' wedding day, for goodness' sake,' he commented. 'Can't we be sociable with each other? Let's celebrate with a drink at the Schooner.'

'All right,' she agreed, taken aback by the suggestion.

'Just as long as you are aware that *I* have been sociable ever since we met.'

He smiled and Jemima thought he should do it more often. Jack was handsome enough when he was serious, but when he smiled...!

'How did the wedding go?' the landlord of the pub shouted across as they seated themselves at a table over-looking the seafront a few minutes later.

As they both opened their mouths to reply Jemima found herself smiling.

'You tell him,' she said, and as Jack gave him a brief description of the event she thought that, whether she liked it or not, there would be a bond between them from now on. Not of liking, or any other sort of rapport, but because their families were joined together by marriage.

It was early evening and already the night was closing in. There was a log fire burning in the grate, the lamps were on and Jemima found herself calming down, which was a state that she hadn't experienced since her first day back in Rockhaven.

'Where do you live?' she asked into the silence that had fallen between them. 'I realised earlier today that I didn't know. I intended asking my mother, but we were so bogged down with getting ready for the wedding that it went clean out of my head.'

Jemima was gabbling and knew it. Jack had that effect on her. She wondered if he was surprised to discover she was curious about him. Yet it was only natural that she should be.

From the moment of their meeting, Jack had known everything there was to know about her but, apart from the information that he was James's son and senior partner at the practice, she knew nothing about the man sitting opposite her.

'I have an apartment, which suits me very well, above the Neptune Gallery just down the road,' he said, and there was indeed mild surprise in his voice. 'It's modern and airy with fabulous views of the Atlantic. Only five minutes walk from the practice and...' He paused and Jemima wondered what was coming next. 'I'm just across from the Severn if I'm needed.'

He gave her a quick sideways glance and went on, 'I know that's something you don't want to talk about, but if you're coming back to Rockhaven, the presence of the lifeboat is something you can't ignore, Jemima.'

'I know that,' she told him stiffly. 'You seem to forget that I was brought up in this place. I just don't ever want to be asked to go out on it again, that's all. Have *you* ever been out when a man has been lost?'

'No, of course not. Your father was the first fatality for a long time.'

'Which doesn't make it any easier to bear.'

'I can believe that, but would you deny the sick or injured your services because of that?'

Jemima was beginning to feel she'd had enough. Who did this man think he was? How dared he start lecturing her about what she should and shouldn't do? They'd agreed that day in his office that lifeboat duties wouldn't be her responsibility when she came back to the practice and now he was trying to persuade her that she was taking the wrong attitude. Well! He could...

He'd seen her expression and was holding up a placatory hand.

'I'm sorry. I deserve to be told to mind my own business. Let's change the subject, shall we?'

'Yes.'

'Right, where were we before I got sidetracked? Oh, yes. I was telling you about the apartment, wasn't I? Dad has been sharing it with me for the last few months. That's how he met your mother. He came for a couple of weeks and stayed on. So, you see, we've both got our homes to ourselves now.'

Jemima nodded, her annoyance waning after his apology.

'And your neighbour? The person you were swimming with the other morning? Where does she live?'

She was doing her own bit to make polite conversation and didn't miss the quick look the question brought forth.

'Emma? She has the apartment below mine. It's a three-storey building.'

'And what does she do for a living?'

Jemima couldn't believe that she was being so nosy. After being at pains to point out that she wouldn't be trespassing in his life, and showing that she resented his interference in *her* affairs, here she was giving him the third degree about the very attractive woman who'd been with him on the beach.

And that, of course, was why. If she'd been flat-chested and spotty, there would have been no need to ask.

'Emma has a gift shop on the main street.'

'Oh, I see.'

Any moment now she was going to find herself asking, And what does she do in the winter? Then it would be her turn to risk a rebuff.

'I have to go,' she said with sudden haste. 'I'm driving back to Bristol first thing in the morning and have packing to do.'

Jack got to his feet.

'I'll walk along with you.'

Jemima opened her mouth to protest and then closed it again. After a short walk along the clifftop she would be entering Surf Cottage as its new owner. It was a thought that brought both happiness and pain. She was home again, but at what cost. Her father dead and her mother with a new husband.

Suddenly company of any kind was welcome. Even that of the man whose every gesture rubbed her up the wrong way. The fates had given her a brother of sorts, she thought wryly as they walked along in the chill night, but he wasn't made in the right mould.

How many times had she wished for someone like that to turn to in her grief? Someone strong and understanding. But, then, Jack couldn't be expected to step into a slot that he didn't even know was vacant.

When they reached the cottage, standing still and silent beneath a starless sky, he said suddenly, 'Are you going to be all right, Jemima? It's been a strange day for all of us.'

She didn't answer, just peered at him in the darkness, straining to see his expression. He took a step nearer and looked down at her upturned face.

Acutely aware of his nearness, she wondered what he would do next, but, typical of him, he merely said, 'So put your key in the lock, then.' When she obeyed, he said, 'Turn it, and switch on the light.'

When she stood framed in the open doorway he reached out and held her for the briefest of seconds.

'I'll see you in four weeks' time, Jemima,' he said, and as she nodded speechlessly he went, a dark shadow disappearing into the night.

When he reached the harbour Jack stood, gazing out to sea.

Was he right in the head, or what? he asked himself on the deserted seafront. Jemima had felt frail and vulnerable in the few seconds that he'd held her, and he hadn't wanted to let her go, but if that was how she'd seemed, it wasn't how she was.

For one thing, she was a doctor. A doctor who in the

past hadn't been afraid to go out with the lifeboat. Even if she'd lost the taste for it now, it didn't alter the fact that she'd done it then.

Then there was the way she'd left her mother to cope at a very bad time. Obviously a toughie when she felt like it. He wasn't sure what he thought about Tom's comments about her. He didn't like the fellow much, but was it a case of no smoke without fire?

Yet he'd asked her to come back into the practice. And at the wedding earlier, and in the bar not so long ago, he hadn't been able to take his eyes off her.

There was irony in his smile. When they'd first met he'd told her half-jokingly that 'big brother' would be watching her, but there'd been nothing brotherly in the way he'd felt tonight.

Yet the smile was fleeting. He'd had a bad experience with Carla and would be slow to risk another. And with the opposite sex in mind, there was the memory of how his mother had treated his father. At least with Hazel, who was obvious and up front with everything, James would know where he stood.

As the peace of the night was broken by the noise of a group leaving a nearby bar, Jack turned and went inside, and as he climbed slowly up to the apartment he wondered how he'd known that Jemima was reluctant to enter the empty cottage.

'So is it true, or not?' Mark Emmerson asked with an edge to his voice when he and Jemima came face to face in the hospital corridor.

Before she could answer, the deputy clinical services manager went on, 'They've just informed me in Personnel that you're leaving. That you're going back to Cornwall. Thanks for telling me.'

Jemima's smile was strained.

'You've been in meetings all day. I couldn't get hold of you and I had to give in my notice today.'

She was thinking that Mark seemed smaller for some reason and not as prepossessing as she remembered. Was it because she'd recently met the pick of the crop when it came to male attractiveness, even though it didn't apply with regard to charm?

Whatever it was, as he stood there, eyeing her questioningly, Jemima knew why she'd never wanted their friendship to be anything other than casual. Mark was a thoroughly decent sort, kind, efficient, the type who wouldn't let one down, but he lacked the magnetism she'd seen in other men.

That she might be comparing him to one in particular was a thought she put to the back of her mind. It was sufficient to know that the grey-eyed, russet-haired hospital manager wasn't for her.

Why it hadn't occurred to her before she didn't know and, she thought guiltily, if she hadn't allowed a casual friendship to drift on to the extent that Mark had seen more in it than there was, he wouldn't be so put out to hear that she was leaving.

'If we could go for a bite somewhere this evening, I'll tell you what's been happening while I've been away,' she suggested placatingly.

He managed a smile.

'All right. What time are you off the wards?'

'I could be free by seven.'

'Shall I call for you?'

Jemima shook her head.

'No. I'll see you at our usual place.'

Ever since coming to the area, Jemima had lived in hospital accommodation. It was cheap, basic and only minutes away from the job. Mark had been to the apartment several times, but tonight she didn't want that. She wanted what might be their last meeting to be on neutral ground. Because he must now be realising that she wasn't serious and he wasn't the type to be kept hanging on.

He'd hinted a few times that he was ready for marriage and so far she'd managed to keep his plans at bay, but now he was going to realise that if he wanted to settle down, it wasn't going to be with her.

The feeling of unreality was still with her. In just one week her life had turned itself round. With Rockhaven and the pink-washed cottage on the clifftop, she was taking a step backwards.

But rejoining the practice, under the eye of the man who'd offered her the position, was stepping into a whole new future, and every time she thought about it she broke into a sweat.

'So, you see, that's the story,' Jemima said later that evening as she and Mark finished their meal at a restaurant that they'd visited several times.

'Yes, so it would seem,' he commented drily.

'You know I've not been happy in Bristol,' she told him. 'My heart has always been back home. But Hazel was always there and I couldn't return to the life I had with her after Dad died. However, things are different now. She's truly contrite and we're closer than we've been in a long time. I think that it's partly because she's found happiness that she wants a better life for me.'

'And what about this stepbrother fellow? What's your opinion of him?' he asked morosely.

'Abrupt. Low on charm. Quick to make judgements.'

'Sounds great!'

'Hmm,' she agreed absently, then said, 'He thinks I only went back to get my hands on the house.'

'And is now of the opinion that he was right?'

'Er…yes…I mean…no.'

'Put your key in the lock,' he'd said. 'Turn it and switch on the light.' Would he have stayed with her until she'd got over her momentary reluctance to enter if he'd thought that?

Mark was getting to his feet. 'What he thinks doesn't really matter, does it? The fact remains that it's over for us, isn't it? You always were like the elusive butterfly. Moving away just as I thought I'd caught you…and now you're going to be out of reach for good.'

'I'm afraid so,' she told him.

It was the longest four weeks Jemima had ever known and she didn't know whether to be glad or sorry. Her mother had phoned a couple of times, mainly to check that she hadn't changed her mind about going back and that the solicitor had sent her the papers to sign.

Jemima could tell that Hazel was happy. From now on they would both be in the places they loved best—her mother amongst the noise and bustle of London and herself perched above the ocean in Cornwall.

And, she thought, both with one of the Trelawney men at their elbow. Though in her case the relationship would be of a less intimate nature than that of her mother.

It was Saturday. At last she was driving south again and this time on arriving she didn't intend to go past the lifeboat house.

Grey November had its grip on Rockhaven now. The sea looked cold and choppy as she pulled up in front of the cottage and daylight was fading fast.

There'd been no heat in the place for a month, so she was expecting a chilly reception from the uninhabited rooms. But to her surprise a fire was burning in the grate and the central-heating boiler was chugging away in the small utility room at the back.

In the kitchen there was a note propped up against the cookie jar on the unit and when she read it Jemima's eyes widened.

'Like Mother Hubbard's, your cupboard is bare,' it said in a bold clear hand. 'Will expect you for dinner at six. Regards, Jack.'

Her spirits lifted. Once again Jack had anticipated her state of mind and she found herself smiling. She was going to have to watch it, or he would be telling her what she was thinking before she'd even thought it.

The last few days in Bristol had been traumatic, with Mark still in the background but not getting involved any more, and the rest of her colleagues happily unaware that she was anything but delighted to be going back home.

If it hadn't been for the fact that she'd kept imagining she heard her father's voice saying, 'Stick with it, daughter,' she might have decided that she needed her head examined for leaving the sane cocoon that life in Bristol had been.

But as she'd read the note everything had slotted into place. Clearly Jack hadn't forgotten that she was due back today and had made sure that the cottage would be warm when she arrived.

Also, he'd guessed that she wouldn't have shopped and was offering to feed her. She hoped all this wasn't on instructions from her mother.

But she had a feeling that Jack Trelawney didn't take orders from anyone. That he was a law unto himself. She would find out if that was the case when she presented herself at the practice on Monday morning.

And in the meantime she was home! Walking from room to room. Savouring the experience and smiling all the time. If her brusque guardian angel had appeared at that moment she would have thrown herself into his arms and hugged him from the sheer joy of being back where she belonged.

By six o'clock she'd unpacked, taken some essential items of food out of the freezer, showered and changed, and was on her way to the apartment overlooking the harbour.

Her previous antipathy towards Jack forgotten in the light of what he'd done to make her homecoming pleasant, there was a lightness in Jemima's step and a new feeling of optimism inside her.

But when she looked up and saw the place in darkness her smile faded. He'd said dinner at six and it was that time now, she thought in puzzlement. Where was he?

A footstep behind had her swinging round expectantly, but it was his neighbour, the raven-haired Emma Carson, who was eyeing her from the pavement outside the Neptune Gallery.

'Aren't you Jack's new relation?' she said as they exchanged glances.

'Er…yes,' Jemima agreed, squirming at the description. 'I was supposed to be dining with him tonight but his apartment is in darkness. Would you happen to know where he might be?'

The other woman shook her head.

'I'm sorry. I've been out all day. You can come up and wait in my place if you like.'

'No, thanks just the same,' Jemima said hurriedly. 'I've a lot to do back at the cottage.'

'What about your meal?'

'I'll get fish and chips on the way back.'

'Jack will be sorry he's missed you.'

'Yes, I'm sure he will, but I'll be seeing him on Monday at the practice.'

'Oh, yes. He told me that you're going to fill the gap,' she said easily.

'Has he really?'

Jemima was tempted to say that she wished he'd also told her where he was likely to be at this moment in time, but Emma seemed like a friendly soul and it wasn't the other woman's fault that she'd arrived tired and frazzled, only to be stood up.

'I'll be on my way, then,' she said. 'If you see him, you might tell him I called.'

'Sure will,' Emma promised, and they went their separate ways.

The fish and chips tasted all right because she was hungry, but all the time she was eating Jemima was conscious of a sense of disappointment.

Had she been looking forward to dining with Jack Trelawney more than she'd realised? she wondered. Where on earth was he? He wouldn't have forgotten the arrangement because he'd taken the trouble to light a fire and switch on the central heating in the cottage. So why had he not been there at his apartment as arranged?

He wouldn't be out visiting a patient as evening visits were dealt with by the emergency GP service. Perhaps his car had broken down somewhere and he was stranded, but surely he would have his mobile with him.

As the evening went on and there was no sight or sound of him, Jemima began to feel worried. Whether she liked the man or not, there was one thing she sensed about him and it was that when he decided to do something, he did it. And he had decided to invite her over for a meal. Heaven only knew why as he'd made it clear enough from the start that he had his doubts about her.

By midnight, even though her unease was increasing Jemima was too tired to wait up any longer. If anything was wrong she would hear soon enough, she thought as she went slowly up the cottage's winding staircase.

In the same second that she switched off the light she heard footsteps on the flagged path below and then her name was called in a voice that was easily recognisable.

When she went to the window Jack was there, a dark shadow looking upwards.

'Hold on, I'm coming,' she called, and when she ran downstairs and opened the door he was leaning against the rose-washed wall looking tired and windblown with a towel of sorts wrapped around his lower left arm.

'Are you going to invite me in?' he asked as she goggled at him.

Jemima stepped back.

'Yes, of course. Where have you been? And what have you done to your arm?'

It was his turn to stare in surprise.

'I thought you would have guessed.'

'Guessed what?'

'Didn't you see that the lifeboat house was empty?'

Her face whitened. 'No, ridiculous as it may seem. I was actually at your place by the harbour but it was dark and I wasn't looking in that direction.'

He sighed.

'And I've been thinking that at least you would know why I wasn't there to play host to you.'

He'd gone through into the kitchen. Unwrapping the towel from around his arm, he was running cold water from the tap over it.

'Let me see,' she said, taking hold of the strong brown

limb which was bleeding from a jagged cut. 'How did this happen?'

Her voice was calm, but inwardly Jemima was shaking. If she'd known where he was it would have been nightmare time all over again.

Yet tonight there was no storm, no raging of the elements to bring the smell of danger into Rockhaven. Though it must have been lurking somewhere or the Severn wouldn't have turned out.

'A call came through from the coastguards that a yacht was in trouble,' he said. 'They'd lost their bearings in thick fog and were low on fuel. There was a teenage girl and her father on board, and to make matters worse the girl thought the old man was having a heart attack. Hence yours truly being present. I'd just got in from lighting your fire and was about to change before I started on the meal when Bill Stennet was banging on my door and that was that.'

'And was it a heart attack?'

'Yes, luckily a mild one. The air-sea rescue helicopter came overhead and once I'd stabilised the fellow they winched us up and flew him to hospital, leaving the Severn to tow the yacht to safety.'

While he'd been explaining the night's events Jemima had been getting together hot water, antiseptic ointment and a sterile dressing, and now she was motioning to the nearest chair.

'Sit down while I bathe your arm,' she told him. 'If you've been at the hospital, why didn't you let them have a look at it? It's a nasty gash, but you might get away without stitching.'

Jack shrugged as if the cut had been the last thing on his mind, but obeyed her orders and sat down on a wooden kitchen chair. As she bent over him, gently bathing the still bleeding cut, she was conscious that his mouth was only inches away from hers. She could feel his breath on her face, smell the tang of salt on him.

When she lifted her head for a second the intensity of his bright blue gaze took her breath away. Desperate to bring balance to the moment, she said quickly, 'So how did you get the cut? You haven't said.'

'I gashed my arm against a piece of sharp metal as I was being winched into the helicopter. It's no big deal.'

'No big deal!' she repeated. 'You are a cool customer! You've been through all that in the space of an evening. Yet you didn't go straight home, which you should have done. Why did you come here first?'

One of his rare smiles flashed out.

'Brotherly responsibilities. I had to check that you were all right. If you remember, your mother left you in my charge.'

'She did not!'

'Well, then, let's just say that I wanted to apologise for not being around when you arrived.'

'You are truly amazing,' she breathed. 'You've been out there, risking life and limb, and you think I would complain about that! You're forgetting that I've been there, done it, and none of it is pleasant.'

'I know, Jemima,' he admitted, serious again. 'Subject closed.'

She was about to fix the dressing on his arm and as she bent over him again the soft swathe of her hair brushed against his cheek. She heard him groan softly.

'What is it?' she asked quickly. 'Am I hurting you?'

He shook his head. 'No. You're just a bit too close for comfort.'

His glance was on the rise of her breasts inside the ivory silk nightgown that was visible where her robe fell away, and as Jemima eyed him in disbelief he got to his feet and planted a fleeting kiss squarely in the middle of her fore-head.

'That's to say thank you for looking after me. It's a novel experience, and before I give in to an overwhelming urge to take advantage of you, I'm going.

'I'll see you on Monday, Dr Penrose,' he said with his hand on the doorhandle. 'And, Jemima, I'm sorry that I brought the lifeboat back into your life on the very first night of your return.'

'It doesn't matter,' she said absently, still bemused by the unexpected kiss. 'Just as long as you and all the others are safe... And, Jack...'

'Yes?'

'*I* ought to be making *you* a meal. You must be starving.'

He shook his head and when he replied his voice had its usual brisk tone.

'No, problem. I had a bite while I was waiting to hear how the guy with the heart attack was. So you can go to bed with an easy mind. Bye for now.'

CHAPTER FOUR

ON SUNDAY Jemima had the fidgets.

'I'll see you on Monday, Dr Penrose,' Jack had said when he'd left the previous night.

There'd been no mention of today as he'd reverted back to a more formal manner, and that would have been fine by her if it wasn't for the fact that he'd been so thoughtful on her behalf in various ways. Not least by calling at the cottage when he'd been tired and hurt before going back to his own place.

Admittedly he'd been on the point of going back into his abrupt shell when he'd left, but it didn't alter the fact that she felt that she should reciprocate by showing some concern on his behalf.

Would he want her knocking on his door, though? If he'd been in a mellow mood yesterday, it didn't mean that today would be the same. But after pacing her small sitting room restlessly, she decided that, whether he liked it or not, she was going to call round and check up on him, and at the same time thank him properly for his thoughtfulness.

She found herself grimacing at the word. Yet, surprisingly, thoughtful was what he'd been, and it would be a cold day in hell when she omitted to thank someone for a kindness.

Though, let it be said, he was the last person she'd ever visualised herself being concerned about. But it wasn't just to thank·him that she intended breaking into his Sunday.

It was to see if he had the same effect on her today as he'd had the previous night. Amazingly, there'd been some sort of chemistry between them. The doubtful and the doubted had for a short time been very much aware of each other and, incredibly, she hadn't wanted him to go.

As Jemima walked along the seafront in the early afternoon she was surprised to come face to face with Emma, walking hand in hand with Will Southern, who helped his parents run a restaurant down by the beach.

'Hi, there,' Emma said in friendly greeting as Jemima approached. 'Did you find out where Jack had got to last night?'

Jemima smiled...for two reasons. Because she liked the woman, and because from the looks of it she was involved with Will, if the way Will was looking at her was anything to go by.

'Yes,' she replied. 'He came round to my place later in the evening to explain what had happened. The lifeboat had been called out and they'd asked for a doctor to be on board.'

The lovebirds were ready to move on and Emma said laughingly, 'That's Jack Trelawney. No fuss. No palaver. Just plain action.'

This time Jack was at home. Jemima could hear footsteps on a wooden floor as he came to answer the doorbell, and she found herself tensing. Would he see this visit as presumptuous? she wondered.

Yet why should he? He came and went as it pleased him at her place, and she *had* been concerned about him the previous night. He was probably expecting her to put in an appearance. Yet he *had* said that he would see her on Monday...not today.

As the door swung inwards she had a half-smile on her face, but it was wiped off when she saw a strange woman eyeing her unsmilingly from inside a spacious hallway.

'Yes?' she said.

'Er…I'm here to see Jack,' Jemima said haltingly. 'Is he available?'

'I'm sure I don't know. But I'll ask him. I'm his wife. And you are…?'

'Jemima Penrose,' she croaked.

'What? That Hazel woman's daughter?'

'I'm the daughter of Hazel…Trelawney, yes.'

She didn't know why she'd given her mother her new title but something told her that this woman wouldn't like it, and as she watched the tightening of a mouth with full red lips Jemima knew she was right about that.

Was she going to be invited in, she wondered, or was she going to be kept standing on the doorstep? Her instincts told her to beat a swift retreat before the situation became any more embarrassing.

But at that moment Jack appeared behind the woman who was claiming to be his wife, and when he saw Jemima standing on the mat his face went blank.

She knew then that this had been a mistake. It would have been better to have taken the hint he'd dropped the night before and waited until tomorrow to speak to him.

'Jemima!' he said in a tone that was neither welcoming nor dismissive. 'Come in. What brings you here?'

The woman with the red lips was eyeing her coldly, and Jemima thought that no way was she stepping over the threshold while she was there.

She threw Jack a smile and followed it by saying quietly, 'No, I won't come in, thanks. I was passing and wondered how the arm was. I also wanted to thank you for lighting my fire.'

If she was disconcerted, he wasn't.

'As I told you last night, it was no problem,' he said levelly, and then in the same tone, which when she thought about it afterwards seemed incredible, he added, 'Allow me to introduce you to Carla. Another relative by marriage.'

The red lips were pouting, the green eyes flashing, and Jemima thought illogically that with a touch of orange blusher she would have put traffic lights to shame.

'How do you do?' she said awkwardly, and then she was turning away, desperate to be out of this weird moment. 'I'm sorry to have interrupted your afternoon,' she told Jack over her shoulder as she reached the first step of the stairs that would take her back to street level.

Jack nodded and Jemima thought dismally that he was agreeing that she had broken into his privacy...and to what an extent!

For the first time since meeting him she'd felt drawn to seek him out. Maybe it was the fleeting kiss that he'd planted on her brow, or his unexpected thoughtfulness in preparing for her arrival yesterday.

Whatever it was, she'd felt that the barriers between them were coming down, and then what had she walked into? He'd kept the fact that he was married a secret. Or had he? The man didn't have to tell *her*, of all people, what was going on in his private life. But why hadn't the abrasive Carla been at the wedding?

Her anger began to kindle. How dared that woman refer to her mother in such a manner? 'That Hazel woman's daughter' had been the label Carla had bestowed on her, and if there was one thing that Jemima wasn't going to allow, it was her mother being referred to in such a manner.

They mightn't be as close as she would like, she thought as she walked the short distance back to the cottage, but no one was going to disparage Hazel while she was around.

Back in her sitting room, she eased herself down onto the wooden settle, which had been her father's pride and joy, and faced up to the fact that she and Jack were back to square one.

He had a wife, for heaven's sake, and she had to admit that she didn't like it. She wasn't pleased to know that he was spoken for, and that was a disturbing thought.

The next thing she knew, he'd be producing offspring! Though it was hardly likely that he would deprive his children from being present at their grandfather's wedding.

The surgery on a November morning was much as Jemima remembered it. The bulk of the holidaymakers had been and gone and those that remained to seek the services of the GPs were local folk and a smattering of visitors who just couldn't tear themselves away from the delights of Cornwall, no matter what the season.

Ann and Chris, the two practice nurses, were the same as before. Both of them were working mothers, like Helen, and elderly Jean Crowther was still keeping a competent eye on the younger and less experienced receptionists.

Bethany had been there to greet her when she'd arrived, and as Jemima had settled herself into the room that until recently had been Tom's she'd wondered where Jack was.

So far there had been no sighting of him, and she wasn't going to ask. That he was the pivot on which the practice revolved was clear. There were signs of his brisk authority all over the place, but none yet of the man himself.

The premises had been redecorated, computers installed, and patients' records had never looked so tidily accessible.

'Jack has just rang in to say he's going to be late. A domestic problem has arisen,' Bethany informed her, as the surgery clock announced that it was eighty-thirty and another day of health care was about to commence.

She didn't mention his wife, and Jemima, still bemused

by the unexpected encounter of the previous day, certainly wasn't going to.

It would be time enough to discuss Carla when he was good and ready to explain why she hadn't surfaced before. And in the meantime, there were patients to see on this first day of the rest of her life.

'So you're back, I see,' her first patient said, and Jemima forced back a groan. Eileen Pringle worked in the lifeboat shop by the harbour and had always made a fuss of her father. A fact that might have annoyed her mother if the two women hadn't been firm friends.

Jemima had glimpsed her in church on the day of the wedding and now here she was, eyeing her sourly and making no attempt to explain why she was there.

'Yes, I'm back, Mrs Pringle,' she said evenly. 'What can I do for you?'

Instead of answering the question, the dubious matron said, 'I usually see Dr Griffiths, but she can't fit me in today.'

'Yes, so I believe. Shall we see if I can help you?'

'I suppose you'll have to,' Eileen agreed grudgingly.

Jemima waited. Minutes were ticking by and they hadn't yet got to the reason for her visiting the surgery.

At last it was forthcoming.

'I've got a hole in my breast,' she said at last.

'I see,' Jemima said carefully. 'I'd better have a look, then, hadn't I?'

There was indeed quite a deep indentation at the side of Eileen's breast near the armpit. Jemima didn't like what she was seeing, but if she was concerned it appeared that the patient wasn't.

'It can't be cancer, or it would be a lump,' she said positively, when told to get dressed again.

'At this moment I'm not sure what it is,' Jemima told her, 'but I intend to find out.'

Jemima was already writing swiftly on the pad of surgery notepaper in front of her.

'I'm requesting that you be given a scan. It will mean a hospital appointment and you shouldn't have to wait long. Once I have the result I'll send for you, Mrs Pringle.'

The woman was getting to her feet, quite unruffled at the prospect of the scan.

'I would have been worried if it was a lump,' she reiterated, 'but this sort of thing is bound to be something and nothing.'

'We'll wait and see, shall we?' Jemima said carefully, and as Eileen Pringle marched out she hoped that the woman was right—that it *was* 'something and nothing'. For her own part, she had her doubts.

In the middle of the morning, conspicuous amongst the rest of those in the waiting room, Jemima espied Zac Abercrombie, an artist of sorts who tried to sell mediocre water-colours on the seafront during the season.

What the bearded, long-haired man lived off during the winter she didn't know, but he had been one of those who'd made himself at home at her mother's expense during the dreadful months after her father's death.

He'd actually wandered into her bedroom one night when she'd been trying to get some sleep above the racket that had been going on downstairs, and though he'd apologised when she'd cried out in alarm, she'd never believed the intrusion had been accidental.

When she flipped through the pile of patients' records in front of her she saw that he'd been allocated to her, so she was about to get another blast from the past.

It was a relief that the rest of those she'd seen had been

strangers. Eileen and Zac were enough to be going on with when it came to familiar faces.

But before she called him in, another familiar face appeared, attached to the body of the man who'd kept his wife under wraps for some reason.

'Sorry not to be here when you arrived,' Jack said briefly, planting his briefcase down on the floor beside him. 'Is everything all right?'

'Yes, of course. It's good to be back here.' She smiled. 'Except for one thing. I'm meeting all the folk I don't want to see. Those I do want to see must all be fit and well.'

His direct blue gaze was fixed on her enquiringly.

'Why? Who have you had in here that you'd rather not have seen?'

'Just a friend of my mother's who observed me with a jaundiced eye, and then my next patient, another acquaintance of Hazel's, is someone rather unsavoury who once came into my bedroom during one of her parties.'

Jack's face tightened. 'The damn cheek! And who might that be?'

'Zac Abercrombie.'

Jack held out his hand.

'Give me his notes. I'll see him. I know the guy and he *is* unsavoury.'

'Thanks. And about yesterday…'

'Forget it, Jemima. There was no harm done.'

'I intruded, though.'

His smile was mirthless. 'Anyone of her own sex would be seen as an intruder by my ex-wife.'

'Your *ex*-wife?'

'Yes. Why?'

'I understood her to say that she was your wife.'

Again the joyless smile tugged at his mouth.

'Carla was always prone to wishful thinking. She wants us to remarry but I've had a bellyful of women.'

'I see,' she said slowly.

She didn't really. She didn't see at all, and in the middle of surgery was hardly the time or place to be asking this surprising man about his personal life. Why had they divorced in the first place, she wondered, and were there any children?

Jack picked up his briefcase and moved towards the door, but he paused and said with brief humour, 'Shall I recommend a barium enema for Abercrombie, a fat-free diet, or twenty-four-hour urine collection?'

Jemima found herself laughing.

'Do what you will. He certainly isn't on my list of those I want to meet up with again.'

But to her surprise the last patient of the morning was. Bill Stennet came in looking somewhat uncomfortable, and as Jemima smiled across at her father's old friend he said, 'It's good to see you behind that desk again, Jemima. It's what your dad would have wanted.'

'Yes, Bill, I think it is,' she agreed, as he cleared his throat awkwardly. 'And what can I do for you?'

'I'm worried about my ticker,' he said. 'But I don't want Jack to know. If he finds out that I'm not as fit as I should be, he'll be banning me from going out with the lifeboat and I don't want that to happen.'

'So why do you think there's something wrong with your heart?'

'Pains in my chest, and I'm out of breath all the time.'

'Take your shirt off and I'll sound you.'

'Any pain in the arms?' she asked when she'd listened to his heartbeat.

The lifeboat coxswain shook his head.

'Good. We'll see what an ECG shows up. I'll see that you get an appointment with all speed. And, Bill...'

'Yes?' he said worriedly.

'If your heart isn't as good as it should be, I can't keep it from Dr Trelawney. It wouldn't be fair to him, the crew or to you.'

He got to his feet and began to button his shirt.

'Aye. I know. Let's hope that it's not as bad as I think.'

When he'd gone Jemima thought that treating the people she didn't know was a lot easier than ministering to those she did.

'I've left you a couple of house calls to make,' Jack said when surgery was over. 'Bethany and I will do the bulk of them. As it's your first day we're going to be kind to you, aren't we, Dr Griffiths?' he said to his gentle partner.

She eyed him whimsically.

'I'm not sure just how kind you think we're being, Dr Trelawney. One of the calls Jemima has been given is Glenda Goodall. I'm told that visiting the lady mayoress can be wearing.'

'I know Ms Goodall,' Jemima told her. 'She was all right when I was here before.'

'That was before she hit the high spots,' Bethany informed her. 'She's a wealthy woman these days and we've heard that she has back problems, but this is the first time she's called any of us out.'

'As long as she's not going to castigate me for past misdeeds, I don't mind what she's like,' Jemima told them with a meaningful glance in Jack's direction.

'Whether they be true or imaginary?' he questioned innocently.

'They aren't true,' she flung back at him, 'so they have to be the result of gossip or, as you say, imaginary.'

And with the thought that he might still have doubts

about her, she went…to a smart house high on the hillside overlooking the sea, where the redoubtable Glenda lived.

'Well! Bless my soul! If it isn't Jemima Penrose!' the mayoress exclaimed when the housekeeper showed Jemima into the ornate morning room where she was resting.

'Morning, Your Worship,' Jemima said laughingly, and the woman on the couch beamed across at her.

'It's made my day, seeing you.' She chuckled. 'Nobody wants to know me these days. I know what they're saying about me, but it's not true. I'm still Glenda Goodall from the Cornish cream shop in the high street. The only difference is that, instead of living in the flat above it, I've decided that I can't take my money with me and have come up here to live in style.'

'But surely you don't make that much money, selling the cream?' Jemima questioned.

'No, of course I don't,' the grey-haired mayoress said. 'An old friend left me all his money and that helped to buy me this place. But, Jemima, I'm not enjoying it because my back hurts all the time.'

'Have you seen either of the other doctors about it?'

Glenda shook her head. 'I've been trying to ignore it. My mayoral duties keep me pretty busy and I don't want to have to cancel any of my engagements.'

'So you've been putting up with it?'

'You've hit the nail on the head.'

'Right. Slip off your robe and I'll examine you,' Jemima told her.

When she'd finished her face was grave. 'There's something not quite right at the bottom of your spine,' she told the woman who'd been her first employer when she'd been after a Saturday job. 'So you know what I'm going to say next, don't you, Glenda?'

The sufferer on the couch sighed.

'X-rays? Scans? And the rest? Is that what you're saying?'

Jemima nodded. 'I know you don't like people who beat about the bush, so I'll tell you what I think it might be.'

The mayoress was eyeing her from beneath lowered lashes.

'Yes, do that,' she commanded.

'I think you might have a tumour on the spine but, for goodness' sake, don't take that as definite. I could be way out in my diagnoses.'

'But you don't think you are?'

'No. I don't.'

'So the prognosis can only get better,' Glenda said prosaically, 'now that you've told me the worst.'

'That's about it.'

The other woman was easing herself slowly off the couch, and when she was upright she said, 'I'd no idea that you were back from wherever you've been hiding yourself, Jemima, but it's great to see you. In the months after you lost your father you had a rough time. Somebody should have sorted your mother out.'

'Maybe,' Jemima said calmly, 'but it's in the past now, Glenda. I'm through it. You know that my mother has married again.'

The mayoress smiled. 'No. I didn't. I must be losing my grip. I knew she was seeing James Trelawney, so I presume that he's the lucky man.'

'Yes. It's James Trelawney, the father of the senior partner at the practice.'

'So you and he are now related?'

'After a fashion.'

Jemima could hear Jack's voice from the previous day, describing his ex-wife as 'another relative by marriage,' and had known that he'd been including her in the description.

'And what do you think of him?' the other woman asked.

'Who?'

'Jack Trelawney, of course. All other men become insignificant when he's around.'

'He's efficient. A man of few words. And he's not sure about me.'

'So why did he take you back into the practice?'

'Good question. I don't know.'

'If he seems abrupt it's because he's had cause to discover that the female of the species is not to be trusted.'

'Not in my case!' Jemima protested.

'No, of course not! I'm talking about Carla, his ex-wife.' Jemima put out a restraining hand.

'Don't tell me, Glenda. I don't want to talk about Jack behind his back.'

'Fair enough,' she agreed. 'You'll find out soon enough anyway. It was a nine-day wonder when they split up. He hadn't been here five minutes when domestic bliss became a "domestic blister" and they were divorced.'

It would have been easy to ask what had happened, but she couldn't discuss Jack with anyone else. She could imagine his cold anger if he found out that she'd got this far in his affairs.

As she drove home that evening Jemima was quietly satisfied. Her first day back at the practice was over and she'd enjoyed it—in spite of Eileen Pringle and the sighting of the seedy Abercrombie. The visit to Glenda had cheered her up, especially when the patient had said as she'd left, 'If you'd been around when they made me mayor I'd have asked you to be my mayoress.'

That would have caused a few raised eyebrows, she'd

thought as she'd driven back to the surgery. To begin with, she was young for such an honour and wasn't popular with everybody in Rockhaven.

But the highlight of the day had been to discover that Jack Trelawney's marriage was really in the past. She would rather it hadn't been there at all, but at least, if what he'd said was correct, it was over.

And why are you so happy about that? she asked herself as she parked outside the cottage. There was a strange feeling in the pit of her stomach as she posed the question. It was only a short time since she hadn't even liked him, and now…

Now what? He was never out of her thoughts. Hadn't been since that first day when he'd rushed to her aid on the seafront and later had dropped the bombshell about his father and her mother.

Was he the reason why she'd agreed to come back? Not for love of the cottage, or her fondness for the place? If it was, she was a crazy woman.

Admittedly, he was less brusque with her than at first, but let her put a foot wrong and he would jump down her throat. He'd said that he'd had his fill of the opposite sex.

And was she going to plead *her* case? Oh, dear, no! Any moves would have to come from him. It was the only way she would ever know what his true feelings were.

Jack had insisted that Carla spend the night at a nearby hotel, which hadn't pleased her. But there had been no way he would have had her in the apartment overnight.

She'd appeared out of the blue on Sunday morning and he'd known immediately that she was up to something. Carla had moved to Scotland with the new man in her life after the divorce and he hadn't expected to see her again.

But something was wrong and true to her custom she

was going to unload it on to him. Where Derry Draycott was he didn't know, but it was clear that they were no longer together.

That she'd opened the door to Jemima had been unfortunate, and he'd wished Carla a million miles away as Hazel's daughter had stood hesitantly on the mat, trying to make head or tail of what was going on.

The comparison between the two women had saddened him. Carla, pushy and confident, in spite of the mess she was in, and Jemima, slender, wraith-like and very beautiful in an understated way.

He'd felt completely fed up after Jemima had gone, but at least he'd put her right today. She knew that his marriage was over. Though why he should expect anything to come of that he didn't know. And did he want anything to come of it? His mother and his wife had left him less than enamoured with their gender.

Yet it didn't stop him from taking a late night stroll towards the headland, even though there was a chilly, boisterous wind. As he looked down at the sea, crashing in turbulent white breakers against the rocks below, he was aware of the lamplit cottage only yards away.

What was she doing? he wondered. Watching television? Reading? Cooking?

It appeared that Jemima was doing none of those things. A soft footfall behind him had him swinging round quickly, and he almost knocked her over the edge of the cliff. But as she cried out in alarm his arms were there, steadying her and clasping her close to his chest.

'My God, Jemima,' he said roughly. 'Why didn't you call out? I nearly pushed you over the edge.'

'I'm all right,' she said, looking up at him from the circle of his arms with the moon reflected in her eyes.

'Yes, I can see that...now. But you might not have been.

I was looking at the cottage and pondering on what you might be doing inside there, and here you are, out in the wild night.'

'I was restless,' she said, looking away from his keen blue gaze.

'So was I,' he admitted, making no attempt to remove his arms, 'and it's a state that I don't like to be in.'

'What do you think is to blame?' she asked softly.

'A lot of things, and I know that what I'm going to do next will certainly not be a cure, but for once I'm going to give in to temptation.'

Jemima was observing him warily. Something in his voice told her what was coming next and she wasn't mistaken.

'Why did you have to come into my life?' Jack murmured with his mouth against hers. 'You're a disruptive influence.' Then he was kissing her like a starving man at a feast.

She pushed him away at last and told him with breathless laughter, 'If this is what I get for almost falling over the cliff, I'll have to do it more often.'

Jack's face was sombre, as if the passion that had consumed him had gone as quickly as it had come. He sighed and her spirits plummeted.

'If I was restless before, I feel a damn sight worse now,' he said flatly. 'Forgive me for behaving like an idiot, Jemima.'

That comment really brought her down to earth. There was anger and hurt inside her as she flashed back at him. 'Thanks for making it clear that you consider having anything to do with me an act of unsound mind.'

'I didn't mean it like that! Can't you see what you're doing to me, Jemima?' he called above the noise of the wind, but either she didn't hear, or didn't choose to hear.

As he gazed bleakly at her departing back Jack decided that he was a fool if he didn't put the brakes on.

Back inside the cottage Jemima stood undecided. She'd marched off in high dudgeon and now she was wishing that she'd stayed and made Jack tell her exactly why he'd kissed her like that.

Her mouth was still warm from his, her blood even warmer from the passion he'd aroused in her, but his cooling off had been much more rapid than hers and she'd felt humiliated.

Maybe the way he'd acted was in keeping with his general attitude towards her. Low on respect, high on arrogance!

She went to the window and looked out. If he was still there she would go and face up to him. Let him see that he had well and truly put his foot in it.

But the moonlit headland was deserted. There was no sign of Jack and with dragging feet she went up the stairs to her solitary bed.

CHAPTER FIVE

THE next few days were mild for November, with blue skies and a calm sea coming and going with its tides. However, kept busy at the surgery, Jemima had little time to enjoy what was typically Cornwall in winter.

Since their memorable meeting on the headland, relations between Jack and herself had been cool and businesslike. Neither of them had mentioned it since, but Jemima knew that, just as what had happened was still starkly clear in her mind, he hadn't forgotten it either.

She could tell by the way he observed her with a sort of watchful intensity when he thought she wasn't looking. As though she were some strange phenomenon that he hadn't quite got the measure of.

It might have been amusing to see the confident·one floundering if she hadn't been facing up to the fact that she was now deeply attracted to him. Attracted to a man who hadn't been slow to take advantage of a close encounter on the windswept headland…in spite of having a predatory ex-wife hovering around.

He never had told her why Carla had been there that day. There'd been no signs of her since, but Jemima was pretty sure that she was the 'domestic problem' that had made him late at the practice on Monday morning.

Maybe one day she might discover from his own lips what had happened between them, although they'd have to be somewhat chummier than at present for that to happen. They seemed an ill-assorted pair, but something must have drawn them together in the first instance.

* * *

Simon Hamer was one of Tom Trask's patients, as were most of those that Jemima was prescribing for.

His records said that the overweight accountant had recently been diagnosed with diabetes and late one afternoon he came in for the result of a blood-sugar test he'd had the previous week.

It was good. It showed that with strict dieting the diabetes was under control and already there was some weight loss according to the scales in the nurse's room.

All of which was good news for the patient, but when a urine sample was taken it showed that there was protein present and the practice nurse who'd been attending him came to Jemima to ask what should be done.

'Protein has showed up twice in this man's tests,' she said 'and yet each time we've sent it to be analysed the reports have been satisfactory.'

'Ask Mr Hamer to come in, will you, Ann?' Jemima said, and when the burly diabetic had seated himself she smiled across at him and commented. 'The weight loss is good, Mr Hamer. The blood-sugar level is under control. But there's this problem of the protein.'

'Nurse tells me that it's happened before and that there was no cause for concern when the results came back, which makes me think that there probably isn't a problem.'

'Sometimes a patient with diabetes has had the illness for quite a while before it's diagnosed, and that can cause protein in the urine. We'll send a sample to be checked once more in the normal way, but if it occurs again during your next visit I'll ask you to do a twenty-four-hour test.'

He sighed. 'It's hell on earth, having no sugar and being on a fat-free diet to get my weight down at the same time.'

Jemima nodded sympathetically.

'This is the first time I've seen you, but the results tell us that you're trying really hard.'

'I am, Doctor,' he said emphatically as he got to his feet, 'and I have to admit I'm feeling better for it.'

'There you are, then, and the more weight you lose, the easier it will be to control the sugar.'

When he'd gone she sat gazing thoughtfully into space. Carla of the red lips had been with Jack when he'd come back from lunch and as far as she knew she was still somewhere on the premises.

Why? Jemima wondered. Was she living in the area? And if she was, why wasn't she letting go? She supposed that an ex-wife had some sort of claim on a man, but if it had been her, she would have wanted to put as many miles as she could between them after a failed marriage. There was nothing as cold as a dead love affair.

As she was tidying up at the end of the afternoon she could hear Carla chatting to Helen in the passage outside her consulting room. Though Jemima couldn't hear what was being said, it was clear from the tone of Carla's voice that she was in a more pleasant mood than the one she'd been in on Sunday afternoon.

Had Carla been at the practice all afternoon? she wondered. If she had, Jack couldn't be that averse to the woman who had once slept in his bed if he could stand her round him for as long as that.

The thought of them sleeping together was something Jemima didn't want to dwell on, and she told herself she was jealous. Ever since that night on the headland she'd wanted Jack, but he'd been showing all the signs of a man who was steering clear of any further dealings with the opposite sex.

With the exception of the one who behaves as if she still owns him, she thought with grim humour. But he wasn't the type to let anyone 'own' him, was he? And where that could have been a comforting thought, it wasn't.

When Jemima went to get into her car at the end of the day she was surprised to see Jack waiting beside his own vehicle, with no sign of Carla in the vicinity.

That gave her food for thought on two counts. The absence of his ex-wife was the first, and the other was the realisation that they'd been in the same building for most of the day and hadn't spoken to each other. If that wasn't proof positive that he was avoiding her, nothing was.

But now, to confound her, he was approaching with his long, easy stride. Looking down at her thoughtfully, he made up for the lack of dialogue between them in one surprising sentence.

'If you've nothing special arranged for tonight, would you like to come round for the meal that I never got around to making for you?'

'I thought that you were...er...that your ex-wife was here.'

'Carla? She's gone.'

Relief washed over her.

'Well, yes, then. In that case, I'd love to.'

'Shall we say half past seven?'

'Mmm. That will be fine. Do I have to dress up?' As he observed her blankly, she went on, 'I mean will there be other people there?'

He almost smiled.

'No. Just the two of us...if that's all right.'

'Yes, of course,' she said easily, ignoring the flutterings in her stomach.

'Bye for now, then,' he said, and as she drove off Jemima was thinking that tonight would be a heaven-sent chance to find out if she did register to any degree with Jack Trelawney.

As he prepared the meal with the same swift precision that he did everything else, Jack was turning over in his mind Jemima's reaction to his invitation.

Obviously she would have known that Carla had been on the premises all afternoon. She liked to be seen and invariably made her presence felt wherever she went.

He had to admire her nerve. She honestly thought that they were going to take up where they'd left off. She was staying in a bed and breakfast place somewhere down the coast, which was rather surprising.

He would have thought she would have based herself in Rockhaven if she was so intent on connecting herself to him again. But she'd let slip that it was the cheapest place she could find. So maybe that was the reason.

After hovering all afternoon, she'd finally gone off in a huff when he'd made it clear that his evening wasn't going to be free. At that point he hadn't even asked Jemima to dine with him, but he'd been intending doing so and he'd decided that nothing was going to prevent him.

As he chopped fresh vegetables and checked that the butter in the pan wasn't heating too fast, he was smiling as he recalled how she'd asked if she should dress up for the occasion.

Once he'd made it clear that Carla was no longer around she'd accepted the invitation willingly enough and he supposed that she might have wondered what form the evening was going to take.

She wasn't likely to be aware that whatever she dressed in had his approval—from the smart suits she wore for the practice, to the green silk 'sea nymph' dress or the bulky waterproof jacket she'd had on that night when he'd suddenly gone crazy with longing at finding her in his arms.

He'd kept at a distance ever since and it hadn't been easy. But having Carla on the perimeter of his life again had helped in a contradictory sort of way. Having her around was a constant reminder of how painful relationships could be.

So in view of all that, why had he asked Jemima to dine with him tonight? Because they were related? Because he wanted to explain why he was behaving like he was? Or was it because he just wanted to be with her?

Unaware that the garment had made such an impression on a previous occasion, Jemima turned up wearing the green silk dress.

'I might have known,' he murmured as she took off her coat in the hallway she'd previously only viewed from the outside.

Dark hazel eyes were fixed on him questioningly.

'Known what? Don't say that I've done something wrong already!'

One of his rare smiles flashed out.

'No, of course not. I was just thinking out loud.'

Thinking that his pulses were racing, along with a quickening heartbeat, which wasn't the best way to start an evening that he'd intended to be cool yet friendly.

'Any news of our parents?' he said with a quick change of subject as he settled her beside the fire with a drink.

'Mum rang yesterday and she sounded on top form. She was never really happy here in Rockhaven. It was too coastal and quaint for someone who'd been brought up in London.'

'But it suits you,' he remarked, with a questioning lift of the eyebrow.

In that moment she was tranquil.

'Yes, it does. I was miserable all the time I was away.'

'So why did you go?'

'I think you know why. Although it will be my mother's version that you've heard. Or that of her friends.'

'Like Zac Abercrombie?'

Her face had clouded.

'No. Actually, I meant her women friends. Eileen Pringle and the others. They were prepared to stand by and watch what she was doing to herself...and me...and let it happen. People like Abercrombie were the hangers-on. The flotsam that hangs around the coastal towns. Psuedo artists and suchlike who saw in my mother a free meal ticket and a bed for the night if they were stuck.'

'Was that how that feckless layabout came to burst into your bedroom?' he asked tightly. 'His feet wouldn't have touched the floor as he made his departure if I'd been around!'

She nodded. 'Yes, but I'd rather not talk about it if you don't mind. I don't expect you to understand what it was like at that time. I was so lonely and sad that...' Her voice trailed away. What must he be thinking of her? It sounded as if she was begging for sympathy, and she'd intended this to be a light-hearted evening.

Jack was observing her soberly.

'I *have* heard other versions regarding your departure from Rockhaven and they *were* prejudiced, I'm afraid. Hazel, I feel, might have wanted to be seen in a good light because she'd met my father and didn't want any blight on the relationship...and I suppose her friends were ready to support her.'

'Don't let's talk about it any more,' Jemima pleaded. 'It's all in the past and, amazingly, my mother and I are on better terms now than we've been for a long time. Consider how she gave me the cottage!'

She wanted to say to him, And if *you* are beginning to think less badly of me, nothing else matters.

But if he were to gaze at her uncomprehendingly, and it was possible that he might, she would want to curl up.

'Of course we won't talk about the past any more,' he said evenly. 'It was my fault for asking if you'd heard from the newly-weds. I invited you round here to talk about a few things, but they were more connected with my past than yours.'

'You mean you and Carla,' she said slowly.

He nodded.

'Yes, but before I do anything else I'm going to serve the meal. Or you'll be thinking I've brought you here under false pretences.'

Jack knew how to cook, she thought as he produced shrimp and bacon salad for starters, followed by steaks with mouthwatering fresh vegetables for the main course and fruit and Cornish cream in brandy-snap baskets for dessert.

But, then, he *would* know how to cook, wouldn't he? Was there anything that he didn't excel at? Charm maybe? He certainly didn't put himself out to captivate.

Maybe he felt there was no need to project himself where her own sex were concerned, that his physical attractions made up for any lack of charisma.

Yet what about marriage? It didn't sound as if he'd been a great success in the minefield of matrimony. But perhaps before the night was over he would tell her what had gone wrong. If he did confide in her, it would be a side of him she hadn't seen before.

He served coffee in the lounge, and as they sat in front of the fire once more, Jemima was so aware of him that her hand shook as she lifted the cup to her lips.

He'd seen the movement and asked, 'What's wrong, Jemima? Are you cold? Or sickening for something?'

She shook her head and the long plait into which she'd braided her hair swung slowly from side to side. When she looked up, Jack's expression told her that he had his answer.

'It's me. Isn't it?' he said. 'You're not comfortable with me? I make you nervous?'

Her smile was wry.

'Yes, you do.'

'Why, for heaven's sake?'

'Don't pretend that you don't know the answer to that!' she exclaimed. 'When I first came back I sensed that you were critical of me for some reason and then, just as I'd adjusted to being low in your estimation, you created a situation where I didn't know if you were attracted to me or if that night on the headland you merely saw me as a body for the use of.'

He had moved across and was standing in front of her.

'If I'd seen you only as a "body", as you so bluntly describe it, would I have left it at that? Don't you think that lust would have been on my mind, rather than the longing that I forced myself to control?'

Jemima was on her feet now and they were standing only inches apart. Near enough for her to pick up the clean male smell of him, and to feast her gaze on golden brows above eyes as blue as the Atlantic on a summer day.

Jack was breathing faster. So was she, and she said softly, 'One of the reasons I came here tonight was to find out where we stand. Are we foes? Friends? Or something more than that?'

He had become very still.

'Do you want us to be more than friends?'

'Do you?' she parried back.

He didn't answer. Just looked deep into her eyes and reached out for her as if he couldn't help himself, and it was as it had been before. Like thirsty travellers who had found an oasis. As Jemima gave herself up to the magic of it, she thought that this was her answer. There *was* chemistry between them. She hadn't imagined it.

But raised voices outside on the seafront were breaking into their absorption in each other and as Jack lifted his head he groaned.

'It sounds as if they're launching the lifeboat. Let's hope that they don't need a doctor on board.' But it seemed that they did.

Bill, now a much happier man since his suspected heart problem had turned out to be a hiatus hernia, was calling from down below, 'Jack! Are you up there?'

Jemima went cold as he gently put her away form him and went to open the window.

'Yes. I'm here,' he called down. 'What is it?'

'An explosion on a German trawler five miles out. It's listing badly and two crewmen are hurt, and according to the coastguards we're going to be sailing into some rough weather.'

'I'm coming.'

He was striding into the hall and picking up his bag almost before he'd finished speaking, and as fear held her motionless he looked at her apologetically.

'Sorry about this, Jemima, when we were just getting to know each other.'

'Don't go!' she choked.

He looked at her blankly.

'What? You of all people should know better than to say that.'

'I of all people know what can happen to those who man the lifeboats!' she flung back at him.

'Maybe, but we'll talk about it when I get back. I have to go.'

If you get back, she thought wretchedly as she watched him sprint along the seafront to where the boat was already being towed down the slipway.

In the process of flinging on waterproofs and a lifejacket, Jack waved once as the craft hit the water and then they were gone. A valiant vessel ploughing through dark waters.

For what seemed like hours Jemima sat huddled by the window. She'd vowed never to go out on the Severn again and thought that way she would never have to go through the horror of seeing any other lives lost at sea.

But what had happened? Terror would be her companion every time a doctor was needed on the lifeboat because she was in love with Jack Trelawney. She wasn't going to be able to cope with it.

The fire in the grate had gone out, just like the fire that had kindled so quickly between them, and in a chilly dawn, feeling cold and miserable, she let herself out of the apartment.

Outside, the open doors of the lifeboat house were an unnecessary reminder of where Jack and the others had gone. Averting her face, Jemima pulled up the collar of her jacket against the wind and began to walk home.

As she walked the last few yards of the coast road Jemima saw it. A bright splash of colour cutting through a choppy sea. The lifeboat was back.

It was a sight that she'd been brought up with and had accepted as part of life in Rockhaven. But since losing her father it had all turned sour and now, if she didn't put Jack out of her life, she would be ruled by its comings and goings again. Like the rest of the women whose men braved the dangerous elements without giving a second thought to their own safety.

Why did she have to be attracted to him? she asked herself bleakly. They were in the same profession, which was good. The rocky start to their relationship had been smoothed out, and life could be taking on a new meaning. But with the spectre of the lifeboat always there, she would have the dread of loss inside her constantly.

Admittedly, he wouldn't be on board as often as her father had been. It would be only when a doctor's skills were needed, but it didn't alter the fact that she was going to be on a knife edge every time he was called out.

Her step had faltered at the sight of the boat and she half turned to go back, then thought better of it. For one thing, Jack might think it presumptuous if he found her waiting for him on the seafront.

Alternatively, if those spell-binding moments in his apartment had meant as much to him as they had to her, to find her there might make him think that she was ready to put the past behind her and put her heart in the hands of the cruel sea again.

And if he thought that, he was wrong. She just couldn't do it. By refusing to allow herself to be on call if the coast-guards asked for a doctor on the lifeboat, she'd thought to have protected herself from further pain. But it wasn't working out like that, Jemima thought as she put her key in the lock of the silent cottage.

She would have to hope that now he'd had time to cool off Jack would decide that those moments in his apartment had been a momentary heating of the blood, and he wouldn't expect anything further from her.

If that was how it turned out, she would feel nothing but relief, she told herself. So why did she turn her face into the pillow and weep as daylight followed the winter dawn?

*   *   *

Incredibly Jack was at the surgery before her when she arrived later looking pale and heavy-eyed, and before she'd even taken off her coat he was there beside her.

'You got home all right, then?' were his first words, uttered with less than his usual brisk confidence.

'Yes, of course,' she said calmly, having no intention of letting him know that she'd spent most of the night huddled by the window in cramped misery. 'Did you get the injured men to safety?'

She had to ask. She was in the situation of saving lives herself, but she didn't really want to know. If Jack began to give her a graphic account of what had happened when they'd reached the stricken ship it would bring back a set of mind pictures that only she had ever seen. Images that she'd faced up to too often for comfort.

But almost as if he guessed what was going through her mind, Jack merely said briefly, 'Yes. We brought them back with us and they were taken straight to hospital with burns and deep abrasions.'

'And the rest of the crew?'

His face tightened.

'We towed the trawler back to port with them still on board. But why ask when you don't want to know?'

'I *did* ask you not to go,' she said stiffly.

'Yes, you did! I wonder what your father would have said if he'd heard that! He doesn't sound like a man who would have condoned self-pity.'

'And what do you mean by that?' she asked slowly.

'*He* was the one who lost his life and, from what I've heard of him, he wouldn't have begrudged the sacrifice. *You* are still here. So, for goodness' sake, Jemima, stop making such heavy weather of it!'

If she hadn't been so hurt and angry she might have seen the unconscious play on words. He was describing her attitude as 'heavy weather'.

She would like to bet that Jack Trelawney had never seen weather as 'heavy' as that on the night when her father had been washed overboard.

The waves had been more than twenty feet high and he'd been swept into the sea with a force that had given him no chance to climb back on board.

And now Jack was castigating her for not being able to forget it. He was doing her one favour, though. He'd just made it easy for her to put the brakes on a relationship that would be a big mistake if it were allowed to proceed.

'How dare you talk to me like that?' she flared. 'Ask Bill Stennet what it was like that night, and you'll know why I'm still traumatised. I was beginning to think that you might be human after all, but I was mistaken. You're arrogant and insensitive. And now, if you'll excuse me, I have my patients to see to!'

As she took her seat behind the desk and waited for the first sufferer to make their appearance, Jemima felt her burning cheeks.

Jack's face had been white as she'd slammed past him. There'd been no heat coming from *him*, just cold censure.

Well, he could keep his opinions, she thought as anger still simmered inside her. At least in the future her anxiety when he went out with the lifeboat would be of the same degree that she would feel for anyone. It wouldn't be tearing her apart because she loved him.

So that was that, Jack thought as he went into his own room. The end of the affair! Whatever had possessed him to say what he had?

It had been a long, stressful night and he was tired. Was that the reason?

No! It wasn't. He'd sparked off at Jemima as he had because he'd been panicking, realising that his involvement with the lifeboat was going to be a major stumbling block to their relationship.

He'd no sooner got his act together regarding all the wrong ideas he'd had about her than it had been her turn to start having misgivings about him. He'd seen her expression the previous night when she'd pleaded with him not to go, and it had filled him with dismay.

How could she ask such a thing of him? He was a doctor, for heaven's sake! Surely she knew that there was always risk in the lifeboat service, and that he was no different to any of the other men—and women—who dropped whatever they were doing when the call came and took to the sea. She'd been one herself, for goodness' sake!

It was a good thing that there was a full waiting room out there to take his mind off what had just happened, but at the first chance he was going to make her see sense.

She had to realize that it was the future that mattered. Their future. And if he couldn't make her see that, then he wasn't the man he thought he was.

Glenda Goodall was Jemima's first patient that morning, and when she came into her consulting room, walking slowly and leaning on a stick, the young doctor put her own troubles to one side in concern for her patient.

Her suspicion that the feisty mayoress might have a tumour at the base of her spine had been confirmed when, opting to have private treatment, Glenda had seen a consultant shortly after Jemima's visit to her home on her first day back at the practice.

Since then she had been successfully operated on and was making a slow but satisfactory recovery. Unless her presence at the surgery today indicated otherwise, Jemima thought soberly.

Glenda was smiling at her expression.

'Don't look so serious, Jemima,' she said. 'I'll be back performing my civic duties before you can blink.'

'So what are you here for, then, Glenda?' she asked with an answering smile.

'To thank you for putting me on the track of my tumour so quickly. As you will have seen from the consultant's report, mine was primary cancer, rather than secondary, so I've been very fortunate.'

'And the mobility?' Jemima asked carefully, having witnessed Glenda's laboured progress.

'Could be better,' she said cheerfully. 'The weight of the tumour had caused some crushing of vertebrae, which has left me with some weakness of the legs, but at least I'm alive and, according to my doctor at the clinic, am likely to remain so. My chauffeur is in the waiting room,' she continued. 'Could you ask him to come in, Jemima?'

Jemima got to her feet.

'Yes, of course.'

When she opened the door and beckoned the uniformed council employee to enter, he got to his feet and, picking up a huge bouquet from on the seat beside him, went to stand beside the mayoress.

Glenda held out her arms and he put the flowers into them.

'These are for you, my dear,' she said, offering them to Jemima. 'Just to say thank you...and will you come and have lunch with me one day when you're free?'

'I'd love to,' Jemima replied as the taste of tears welled up in her throat. 'Seeing you today, Glenda, has helped me to get one or two things in perspective.'

When the older woman had made her painful exit Jemima allowed herself a moment's thought. Had it needed Glenda to remind her that she could do nothing for the dead? That it was the living who mattered? Was that what

Jack had been saying in that tight, hateful voice when he'd berated her earlier?

But she *was* thinking about the living. That was why she couldn't contemplate giving her heart to a man who might be taken away from her as her father had been.

Which all went to show that she should have fallen in love with a man who had an uncomplicated job. Like a greengrocer, or a plumber!

As she buzzed for the next patient to present themselves Jemima looked up to see Emma smiling at her from the doorway, and once again she made herself tune into the needs of those who had come to consult her.

CHAPTER SIX

EMMA had an older woman with her and when they had seated themselves she explained, 'I've brought my mother to see you, Doctor. She's here on sufferance as she thinks I'm fussing about nothing.'

The older woman sighed.

'I'm quite capable to speaking for myself, Emma,' she said tightly, and turned to Jemima. 'I went to America a few weeks ago to visit my brother and his wife. While I was there he insisted that I have my blood pressure checked on a home testing kit. I wasn't really bothered as it has always been spot on, but to my surprise the reading that came up was quite high. Needless to say, I decided that the machine must be faulty,' she said decisively.

'However, when I got back and mentioned it to Emma she insisted that I have it checked again…and that's why I'm here.'

'And rightly so,' Jemima told her. 'Have you had any headaches lately?'

Mrs Carson shook her head.

'No.'

'Do you lead a stressful life?'

'I suppose you could say that. I work for the church. Help various charities on a voluntary basis, such as meals on wheels, cancer care and the NSPCC, and I'm chairwoman of the Townswomen's Guild, which does mean that I rarely have a minute to spare.'

Jemima smiled across at the elderly human dynamo.

MILLS & BOON®

An Important Message from The Editors of Mills & Boon®

Dear Reader,

Because you've chosen to read one of our romance novels, we'd like to say "thank you"!

And, as a **special way** to thank you, we've selected <u>two more</u> of the <u>books</u> you love so much **and** a welcome gift to send you absolutely <u>FREE</u>!

Please enjoy them with our compliments...

Tessa Shapcott

Editor, Mills & Boon

P.S. And because we value our customers we've attached something extra inside...

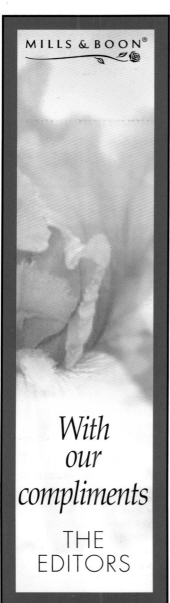

MILLS & BOON®

With our compliments

THE EDITORS

alidate your
ift "Thank You"

Gift Seal from the front
provided to the right. This
receive two free books
Austrian crystal necklace.

etails on the card, detach
post it back to us. No stamp
u two free novels from the
These books have a retail
urs to keep absolutely free.

/e hope that after receiving
t to remain a subscriber. But
tinue or cancel, any time at
no risk invitation? You'll be

n is guaranteed

to buy anything. We charge
luctory parcel. And you don't
m number of purchases – not
of readers have already
ader Service™ is the most
ing the latest new romance
ilable in the shops. Of course,
ur home is completely FREE.

Shapcott

Mills & Boon

omplimentary book mark

The Editor's "Thank You"

You'll love this exquisite gold-plated necklace with its 46cm (18") cobra linked chain and multi-faceted Austrian crystal which sparkles just like a diamond. It's the perfect accessory to dress up any outfit, casual or formal. RESPOND TODAY AND IT'S YOURS FREE.

Not actual size

Yes! Please send me my two FREE books and a welcome gift

PLACE EDITOR'S "THANK YOU" SEAL HERE

Yes! I have placed my free gift seal in the space provided above. Please send me my two free books along with my welcome gift. I understand I am under no obligation to purchase any books, as explained on the back and opposite page. I am over 18 years of age.

M2EI

BLOCK CAPITALS

Surname (Mrs/Ms/Miss/Mr) _____Initials_____

Address_____

_____

_____

_____Postcode _____

HOW THE READER SERVICE™ WORKS

Accepting the free books places you under no obligation to buy anything. You may keep the books and gift and return the despatch note marked "cancel". If we don't hear from you, about a month later we will send you 4 brand new books and invoice you just £2.55* each. That's the complete price – there is no extra charge for postage and packing. You may cancel at any time, otherwise every month we'll send you 4 more books, which you may either purchase or return – the choice is yours.

*Terms and prices subject to change without notice.

The Reader Service™
FREEPOST CN81
CROYDON
CR9 3WZ

NO
STAMP
NEEDED

'In other words, there aren't enough hours in the day?'

'Yes, and Emma doesn't seem to realise how busy I am...dragging me here when I should be serving on the W.V.S. counter at the hospital.'

Said daughter rolled her eyes but made no comment as her mother took off her jacket, and Jemima hid a smile. But her face was serious when she'd done the reading.

Two pairs of eyes were fixed on her expectantly when she looked up, one of them anxious and the other calmly confident.

'Your blood pressure *is* up, Mrs Carson,' she told Emma's mother. 'You know that the reading gives us two figures and it's the lower one that we're most interested in, but there's also cause for alarm if the top one is over a hundred and fifty—and yours is a hundred and seventy-nine.'

Seeing her expression was like watching the air oozing out of a pricked balloon, Jemima thought, yet it made a change to have a patient who thought there was nothing wrong with them!

'So what happens now?' Mrs Carson asked in a much less confident manner.

'I want you to come in for the next three weeks to have your blood pressure checked by one of the practice nurses, who will report back to me. It's possible that you were stressed when you had it tested in America and that you're wound up today because Emma has insisted on bringing you. Maybe the next time it will be all right.'

'And what if it isn't?'

'We'll do another couple of tests and if there's still a problem I'll have to put you on medication. You may not think so at this moment, but you've been lucky. High blood pressure can be an unseen killer, but you had a relative who was keen to try out his gadget…*and* you have a caring daughter.'

'Yes, I have,' she agreed in a low voice, and turned to her daughter. 'So I'm not invincible after all.'

'Which of us is, Mum?' Emma said, giving her a hug.

When Emma had ushered her mother through the door she turned back and said quickly, 'Tell me to mind my own business if you like, but I thought you might like to know that a certain person known to us both is having ex-wife trouble. The boy is coming down from Scotland in the near future and she's wheedling Jack to allow them to stay with him as *she's* in some sort of bed and breakfast place.'

'Are you coming, Emma?' her mother was calling.

Jack's likable neighbour glanced over her shoulder in the direction of the voice.

'Must go. Mum's getting fidgety.'

When they'd gone, Jemima's thoughts were in chaos. Jack had a child he'd never thought fit to mention. What sort of a father was that? And why wasn't the boy living with one or the other of his parents?

It would seem that Carla had more claims on Jack than she'd thought. He was obviously nobody's pushover, but this item of news took everything to a new dimension. How could he just ignore the mother and child?

Had he been thinking of his responsibilities when he'd held her in his arms and kissed her until she'd been limp and unresisting?

It would appear not. The man was a law unto himself and the more she heard, the more the need to stay clear of him was becoming the only way to stay sane.

Brisk and efficient he might be at the practice and when called upon to accompany the lifeboat, but was Jack a loose cannon beneath it all?

She could understand him not inviting his ex-wife to the wedding, but to deprive James of the pleasure of having his grandson present was too bad.

Yet for someone who had decided that their lives weren't going in the same direction, Jemima lost no time in way-laying Jack the moment that surgery was over.

'Have you a moment to spare?' she asked from the door-way of his consulting room.

He was studying a patient's records but looked up at the sound of her voice.

'Of course. Take a seat.'

Perching herself firmly on the chair opposite, and with all guns firing, she said, 'I believe you have a son, Jack.'

'Really? And who told you that?'

'Does it matter?'

'It might, seeing that it isn't so.'

'I'm not with you,' she breathed.

'Obviously.'

'So who is the boy coming down from Scotland?'

There was grim mockery in his smile.

'He's Carla's son, not mine. I'm bogged down with re-lations through marriage.'

Ignoring that comment, she went on to say, 'So you and she have no children?'

'No.'

'She's been married before?'

'No.'

'So where——?'

'So where has young Callum come from, you're asking?'

This is the moment where he tells me to mind my own business, Jemima thought, and I wouldn't blame him if he did.

But he didn't. Getting to his feet, Jack walked across to

the window and stood looking out towards the windswept shore.

'I think I once told you that I've had my fill of devious women,' he said levelly. 'First my mother, who made my father's life hell with her infidelities. Then, as if I hadn't seen enough of cheating and deceit, I married Carla, who turned out to be no better, although in those days she was less demanding, a nicer person altogether, or so I thought. She was head receptionist at the practice in Portsmouth where I worked previously, and I saw her as efficient, attractive, slightly pushy, but not so much that it put me off.

'What I didn't know when we got married was that having affairs was a way of life to her and that the current one had been running parallel with our engagement. I discovered a letter from the other man that gave the game away. Which makes yours truly look rather foolish, doesn't it? We moved to Rockhaven just before the wedding and there were some raised eyebrows when the doctor's wife departed almost as soon as she'd arrived.'

Jemima's heart had been aching for him while he'd been making the toneless explanation. It fitted in with what Glenda had said that day when she'd visited the mayoress.

'And the child?' she questioned softly.

'Chastened by the fact that I'd divorced her, Carla went to live with the fellow and Callum is theirs. The three of them have been living in Scotland where the boy's father comes from, but a short time ago she left in a huff and since then has been hovering on my doorstep. She's just discovered that her partner has to go into hospital and Callum is coming to stay with her until he's well again. For some cockeyed reason she wants us to be a threesome while he's here. Which is crazy when I hardly know the child. I feel that she's hoping I might get to like the arrangement.'

'And does she expect the little boy's father to agree to that?'

'If I know Carla, he won't know anything about it until he's discharged, and she's expecting him to be hospitalised for a few weeks.'

'How old is Callum?' Jemima asked as the implications of what she'd just been told began to sink in.

'Twelve months old, and as I'm sure you'll agree, it's what's best for him that counts.'

'Absolutely,' she agreed. 'But how could a mother leave a child of that age?'

'How could a mother leave a child of *any* age?' Jack said grimly. 'Both you and I had mothers who were less than satisfactory, but at least they stayed around. Although, with mine, it was a miracle that she did.'

'So, you see, Jemima,' he said, with his face still turned to the window, 'we both have the past to haunt us. In different ways maybe, and in your case on a much more tragic level. Which does allow me to understand why you don't want to leave yourself open to any more heartache.'

She couldn't keep her distance any longer. Common sense was being replaced by the need to hold this man whose confidence and style were the products of bitter experience.

Walking swiftly across the room, she took his arm and pulled him round to face her.

'I can see why you're wary of my sex,' she said softly, reaching up to cup his face between her hands. 'You've been hurt by the two women who should have given you tenderness and love. I would never do anything like that to you, no matter what you've heard about me.'

'I know that now,' he said wryly, 'but—'

Jemima put her finger against his lips.

'No "buts", if you don't mind. Can't we be positive?'

Jack's arms were around her now, the male hardness of him telling her that his responses to her nearness were as 'positive' as anything she was ever likely to experience.

For a timeless moment they'd forgotten that not far away were practice staff likely to burst in on them any second, and a knock on the door had them breaking reluctantly apart.

It was one of the receptionists to say that a medical rep was waiting to see Dr Trelawney as soon as he was free.

'I'll be with them in five minutes,' he said, and as she went bustling off he turned to Jemima.

'Considering that you're unhappy about my serving with the lifeboat when needed, and I'm about to get myself involved in a messy situation with Carla if I'm not careful, would you say that the interruption was opportune?'

Her face became blank. What was this? The brush-off?

'Yes. I suppose you could say that,' she said casually, 'and as you have someone waiting, I'll be off.'

'Wait, Jemima!' he cried as she went through the doorway, but she didn't respond.

She had calls to make and the sooner they were done the sooner she could get back to the cottage for a respite before late afternoon surgery.

As she drove along the coast road to visit a sixty-year-old woman who had awakened that morning to extreme dizziness and was consequently unable to stand up unaided, Jemima was aware that although Jack had been forthcoming about what was going on with Carla, he hadn't said what he intended doing about it.

It would be incredible if he let her manipulate him to the

extent that she was suggesting, no matter how concerned he was for the child.

Was it possible that he still had feelings for his ex-wife, as he wasn't exactly refusing to have anything to do with her, in spite of how she'd behaved?

Jemima brushed a strand of hair from her brow wearily. Many questions plagued her mind, but the one that needed answering the most was where were they heading, Jack and herself.

The second they touched the spark was there, each answering the need in the other. Yet no sooner had they melted into each other's arms that one or the other of them was drawing back, wary of further hurt.

Margaret Selby's records showed that she rarely had cause to consult her GP. But today was a different matter. Jemima found her slumped in a chair in her sitting room with her head back against the cushions and her eyes closed.

A neighbour had let her into the big stone house which had once been a vicarage and told her, 'I'll be next door if you need me, Doctor.'

'Yes. Thank you,' she said as she pulled up a chair to sit opposite the patient.

'How long have you been having the dizziness, Mrs Selby?' she asked as the woman opened her eyes.

'It started in the night. I got up to go to the bathroom and I was falling all over the place,' she informed Jemima.

'Right. I'm going to look at your ears first to see if you have an infection,' Jemima told her. 'Any problem with the ears can affect the balance.'

'They don't hurt, but they've felt funny ever since I flew back from my daughter's in Australia last week,' Margaret said.

Taking an otoscope from her case, Jemima examined the ear canal and eardrum, and when she'd finished she shook her head.

'There's no visible sign of inflammation, Mrs Selby, but there may be infected fluid in the ear canal. Long flights can affect the ears. Did you have any problems with them while you were airborne?'

'They hurt a lot when we were going up and coming down.'

'Hmm. It could have been the flight but, tell me, have you had a flu bug recently, or anything similar?'

'Yes,' Margaret said immediately. 'I was ill with a flu-type virus just before I came home.'

'That could be it. A combination of the two. The flight and a virus. I suspect that you might have labyrinthitis.'

'What's that?'

'Inflammation of the fluid-filled chambers in the inner ear, which can affect balance. I'm going to put you on an antihistamine drug and if that doesn't clear it up I'll arrange for you to have X-rays and various other tests. In the meantime, stay still as much as you can until the treatment takes effect. Will your neighbour be able to stay with you until then?'

The other woman smiled.

'Yes. Maxie and I look after each other. We both live alone.'

Jemima had finished her house calls by half past two and after a snack back at the cottage she went for a short stroll on the headland.

It was a mild day, with a blue sky dotted with fluffy white clouds, and the sea only boisterous when it hit the rocks below.

The calendar on her kitchen wall said that November was almost spent and that Christmas was coming fast on its heels. What sort of a festive season would it be for her? she wondered as she watched the breakers come in with relentless regularity, and would 'festive' be the right word to describe it?

It wouldn't be anything new if it wasn't. She'd spent the last two Christmas holidays working at the hospital in Bristol. But at least this year she was home, in the place she loved best, and if the fact that she was in love with a man who had so many sides to him she couldn't count them brought joy or misery, she would have to accept it.

According to what Jack had said, it looked as if Carla would be bringing her child to Rockhaven for some weeks, which could run into the Christmas period. If he did become involved with them, what of herself? Was his scheming ex-wife planning a 'happy families' Christmas?

From what she'd seen of her, the woman was an attention-seeker and maybe the attention had been in short supply. Being engaged to a busy GP had left her with too much time on her hands. Whatever the reason, it took some believing that a woman with Jack Trelawney in her life could look at another man.

As she began to retrace her steps back to the cottage to get ready for the second surgery of the day, Jemima was wishing that she'd told him how she felt when they'd held each other close in his consulting room.

Yet maybe it was as well she hadn't. He'd been quick enough to remark that the interruption had done them a favour. If he'd wanted her to know that he wasn't too happy about how their relationship was developing, he couldn't have made it clearer than that.

Eileen Pringle, Hazel's friend, came marching in during surgery, still on the offensive but slightly less acerbic, having discovered that the hole in her breast, which she'd been so sure wouldn't be cancer, was indeed the dreaded illness.

Jemima had received a report from the consultant at the cancer clinic she'd been referred to, which said that she'd been prescribed an anti-cancer drug for a tumour that was pulling at tissue and creating the sunken area at the side of her breast.

What she'd been like when told the diagnosis Jemima didn't know, but it must have been a great shock in view of Eileen's assumption that it had to be a lump for it to be cancer.

'This drug I'm on is making me feel sick and dizzy,' she said when she'd seated herself. 'Can you give me something for it, Jemima?'

She nodded sympathetically.

'Yes. I'll give you some anti-sickness tablets. There are always side effects with anti-cancer drugs, Eileen. If it gets really bad ask for an appointment with the consultant, but hopefully these will do the trick.' She turned to her computer. 'I was sorry to hear that the problem was more serious than you thought.'

The prickly matron cocked her head to one side and observed her with piercing grey eyes.

'You knew what it was, didn't you, when I was going on about it not being cancer? Why didn't you tell me?'

'Because at that time there was nothing to tell. Would you have wanted me to fill you with alarm before you'd got an appointment to see someone? It *is* usually a lump with breast cancer, but not always, and I wasn't going to take any chances.'

'So I suppose I should be grateful,' Eileen said grudgingly.

Jemima smiled.

'I was just doing my job.'

Clutching the prescription, the other woman got to her feet. Avoiding the young doctor's quizzical hazel gaze, she said, 'Well, I *am* grateful, and I shall tell your mother so when I see her...that's if I ever see her again. Is she coming back for Christmas?'

'I really don't know,' Jemima told her, 'but I'll let you know if she is.'

'Yes, do that,' Eileen said, and off she went.

'What's the joke?' Jack asked when he went in and found her smiling after Eileen's departure.

'I've just won over another of those who liked me not.'

'Huh?'

'Eileen Pringle, an old friend of my mother's who gave me the sharp end of her tongue on my first day back here.'

'I see. And the others that you've charmed?'

'Just one. Hopefully...you.'

It was his turn to smile.

'I like your choice of words. Charmed is something that I rarely am, but I have to admit that when it comes to you I have to keep a hold on my emotions.'

'So I've noticed.'

'What? How you affect me?'

'No. How good you are at pushing me away after you've aroused me.'

The smile had gone.

'Have you, or have you not, made it clear that you don't want to make any commitments that might bring sorrow?' he asked levelly.

'Er...yes.'

'Well, then. We're talking about a man who has a job that sometimes leads him into dangerous waters. Is he the one for you, Jemima Penrose? I think not.'

Without allowing her the right of reply, he went back to his own room and there was no way she was going to run after him to plead her cause. He was applying the same sort of cold logic to their relationship that he applied to everything else.

What was the matter with him? Jack Trelawney thought as he raked his fair hair with a frustrated hand. For the first time in his life he'd met a woman who excited him, enthralled him, was clever and brave and honest, and he was dithering about like a nervous teenager.

The answers weren't hard to find. He wasn't going to forget in a hurry how the sight of the lifeboat and its elderly coxswain had affected Stephen Penrose's daughter that day on the seafront.

Only someone who'd been in Jemima's situation on the night she'd lost her father would understand her reluctance to become involved in that sort of scenario again. And, if he really wanted her, surely the answer was to tell the lifeboat service that they would have to find another GP to go out with them when medical help was needed.

But it wasn't that easy. Bethany was too frail for that sort of thing, and Jemima was the only other GP in the practice. With regard to himself, he was the ideal person. Strong, resilient, used to the sea with all complexities…and with no one, apart from his father, to grieve if it took him into its mighty depths one day.

It was a fact that all who sailed on the lifeboats had to face, that one day they might die in the service that they so willingly gave. The women who loved them accepted it.

So had Jemima, who'd also been brave enough to sail with them, but she'd been too close when her father was lost and now she had to live with the horror of it.

She was right to feel how she did about their relationship. Friends rather than lovers was where they should be heading.

All very praiseworthy sentiments, but how easy was it going to be to put them into practice when they worked in the same place and their respective parents had just married each other? And what was going to appease the ache inside him every time he was near her?

Christmas was coming. One of the most romantic times of the year. He would have to watch himself, or the cool and capable image that he liked to portray would be a thing of the past.

Deep down he knew that he wanted to spend it with Jemima but, as well as everything else, there was Carla hovering in the background, pushing for her and the boy to stay with him. And what was she planning to do after that?

He'd soon sent her packing when he'd found out that during their engagement she'd been sleeping with Derrick Draycott, a medical rep who'd frequently called at the practice in Portsmouth. The memory of that time always brought a bitter taste to his mouth.

Draycott had been a flashy dresser with long black hair tied back in a ponytail and a line of patter that would have sold ice cream to the Inuits. Obviously a more interesting prospect than an overworked GP.

But to Carla, who had proved to have a skin like a rhinoceros and no morals, that was all a blip in the past and he had a gut feeling that she was going to be a nuisance in the coming weeks.

Why she'd left Derrick and the child she wasn't prepared to say, and where normally he sorted problems with brisk competence, he was undecided what to do about her.

Putting the problem of Carla and her child to one side, he allowed his thoughts to return to Jemima.

He'd had his life organised. The elegant flat beside the harbour. The practice that was running on oiled wheels, and his father now settled into a new marriage with Hazel.

But it had all changed on the day when he'd looked down at a slender woman with pale skin and hair of burnished brown lying limply at his feet.

He'd heard about her, of course, but hadn't expected to make her acquaintance under such circumstances. She was Hazel's daughter, who had left her mother to cope in the painful early days of widowhood, and out of the blue had gone to do her own thing. He'd thought at the time that maybe she'd had her reasons, but that it seemed a callous thing to have done.

Then he'd had an earful about Jemima one night when Tom had been partaking of wine. How they'd worked together at the practice and how she'd led him on to believe they could have a future together, only for him to discover that she'd no feelings for him whatsoever when he'd proposed.

He hadn't liked the fellow much, but had sympathised with his hurt. His story had seemed to fit in with what he'd already heard about her and, though he didn't like to admit it, his attitude towards her in those first days had been brusque to say the least.

But he'd soon found that she was nothing like he'd imagined, and the more he got to know her, the more he knew that a woman like Jemima would never associate with a nasty piece of goods like Trask. 'Sour grapes' was the phrase that sprung to mind.

With a sigh he reached for his jacket. It had been a long and busy day, and in the middle of it there'd been a magical moment that he'd wanted to go on for ever...and what had he done? Put the finger of doom on it. He was crazy.

Tomorrow was his day off. Maybe a drive into Penzance to do some Christmas shopping would put him in festive mood, but he doubted it.

An emergency just as she was ready to go had Jemima turning back. She'd heard Jack leave and was about to do likewise when one of the receptionists rang through to ask if she would see a mother and child who had a problem.

'Yes, of course,' she told her. 'Send them in.'

Her eyes widened when she saw what the problem was. A little girl, who was holding tightly to her mother's hand, had a saucepan stuck on her head.

'Kirsty was watching me get the evening meal ready,' the woman said, 'and wanted to pretend that she was cooking, too. So I gave her a couple of old pans to play with...and you can see what's happened.'

'Indeed I can,' Jemima murmured. With a smile for the child, who was eyeing her fearfully, she said gently, 'Do you think you can keep very still while I see if I can get it off, Kirsty?'

The little one shrank back against her mother and it was obvious that the efforts that had been made to remove the saucepan before she'd come to the surgery were still clear in her mind.

'I couldn't budge it,' the woman said, 'and the more I tried the more she screamed.'

Jemima was eyeing the child thoughtfully. Fortunately

Kirsty had plenty of curly hair which would stop too much
bruising of the scalp and might create a better surface than
sparse locks or bare skin to try to ease the saucepan off.

The receptionist had appeared in the doorway with a foil-
covered packet in her hand.

'I bought some butter at lunchtime,' she said. 'Do you
think we could grease it off?'

'Maybe,' Jemima said. 'If we spread the butter all round
the edge of where the pan is resting it might come off more
easily, but I'd have to pull it further down to get it onto
the greasy part, which could make matters worse, and I
don't think that Kirsty will be too keen on the idea.'

'Why don't we take her into the waiting room where the
television is?' the receptionist suggested. 'There are cartoons on at the moment and if we can distract her for a
little while…'

The next few minutes were nerve-racking as Jemima
tried to ease the saucepan off the child's head amidst al-
ternating screams of protest and giggles at the cartoons.

Just as Jemima was deciding that a visit to Casualty was
called for, the saucepan came off, leaving the three women
limp with relief and the child shaking her curly locks glee-
fully.

Driving home at last, the funny side of the incident was
uppermost in her mind, and when her mobile rang and she
pulled to the side of the road Jemima was laughing.

Jack's voice came through when she answered. He said,
'You sound in relaxed mood.'

'I am…now,' she told him, 'but I was somewhat traumatised earlier.'

'Not something I've done again?' he asked warily.

'No,' she said, the amusement still there. 'It wasn't anything to do with your disruptive influence. I've been wrestling with a saucepan.'

'Really? Am I supposed to know what that means?'

'No,' she said again. 'You're not, but I'll explain. I've spent the last half-hour with a child who had a saucepan stuck on her head.'

'Oh, dear! And how did you manage to get it off?'

'With patience, fortitude, some cartoons and a packet of butter,' she gurgled.

'Right. Though I'm still a trifle confused.'

'I was in an absolute lather by the time I got it off,' she told him, 'and the child's mother and one of the receptionists who was still there were also in a state, but Kirsty recovered within seconds.'

'No pain or bruising?'

'One would have thought so, but not from the looks of her. Fortunately she had plenty of hair. But enough of my pan-handling. What did you want me for?'

'I'm going to Penzance tomorrow to do some Christmas shopping,' Jack said warily. 'Do you fancy joining me?' He'd said it on impulse, and as soon as the words were out had known how desperate he was to spend some prime time with her.

'I'd love to,' she said immediately, 'but it's your day off…not mine.'

'It's late night shopping,' he persisted. 'We could meet up after you've finished surgery.'

'Yes, all right.' Jemima glowed as her recent gloom melted away. 'Where shall we meet…and what time?'

Jack was waiting for her at the arranged place in the town centre, standing tall and straight beneath Christmas lights that made his hair glint gold.

Jemima found herself breathing faster at the sight of him. He looked trim, wholesome and very desirable. The kind of man who would always make heads turn.

She'd rung through on her mobile to say that she was on her way and now, with just an hour to the shops closing, she'd arrived.

The moment she pulled up he was beside the car, and she saw from his smile that tonight he was wearing yet another mantle. Gone was the brisk senior partner and the cool stepbrother. There was a warmth in his bright blue gaze that was making her colour rise and she thought, What's it to be tonight?

Casual acquaintances? She hoped not. Friends? It was better than nothing. Lovers? Yes, please!

She was wearing a long black coat with smart ankle boots and a big white fur hat, and as he helped her out of the car his smile deepened.

'Julie Christie, eat your heart out,' he teased. 'I feel as if I should either be pulling a sledge or wearing an astrakan hat…or both.'

As she laughed up at him Jemima was totally happy. The evening was half-gone because of her duties at the surgery, but she intended to make the most of what was left of it.

She didn't know why Jack had asked her to join him, especially after his abrupt dismissal of those brief moments they'd spent in each other's arms in his consulting room.

But the fact remained that he had, and these days every moment spent with him was making her realise just how much she was beginning to care for him.

'I've done most of my shopping,' he was saying as he tucked her arm in his, 'so in the time that's left we'll concentrate on yours, shall we?'

Jemima nodded. If he'd suggested they play tick around

the bus station, or do a tango in the main square, she would have agreed.

When he told her that he'd booked a table for them to have supper in the town's best restaurant her eyes sparkled. This is turning out to be a night that dreams are made of, she told herself. Yesterday's frets are over and tomorrow can take care of itself, but tonight I'm going to take hold of the moment.

As they strolled around the shops Jack's eyes were on her face. Jemima was more beautiful tonight than he'd ever seen her. There was colour in her cheeks and her mouth was tender. He hoped it might have something to do with him.

Their differences seemed as nothing at that moment, and as his mood turned itself to hers he gave himself up to the pleasure of being with her.

They'd eaten a leisurely meal, with the candles on the table casting flickering shadows on their faces, toasted each other with crystal wineglasses clinking, and as far as Jemima was concerned it could have gone on for ever.

Jack got to his feet at last. 'We've got to make tracks, Jemima,' he said regretfully, 'or there'll be no doctors on duty in the morning. It's Bethany's day off tomorrow, don't forget.'

She nodded obediently and, still wrapped around in enchantment, slipped her arms into the long black coat which a waiter was holding for her.

Outside on the pavement Jack realised that he'd left his car keys on the table and went back for them. It was as she stood shivering in the cold night air that it happened.

A group of teenage girls had come out of a nearby bar and were larking about at the edge of the pavement. As she watched, one of them ran out into the road, intent on joining a group on the other side.

There was a car speeding towards her but she didn't seem to be aware of it. Her friends had seen it, however, and a shout went up.

The girl stopped and, swaying on her feet, eyed them groggily but didn't move, and as the vehicle screeched to a halt the force with which he'd braked flung the driver forward and his head went through the windscreen.

'Oh! No!' Jemima gasped. 'He can't have been wearing a seat belt.'

'See to the girl while I take care of the driver,' Jack's voice bellowed in her ear, and as Jemima ran to the teen-ager who'd been hit by the front fender, he told the on-lookers who were surging forward anxiously, 'Leave it to us, please. We're doctors. Someone phone for an ambu-lance and tell them to be quick.'

'Very quick,' he muttered as he bent over the uncon-scious driver.

The man's breathing was very shallow and his neck, which was bleeding badly, was at an awkward angle. Jack opened the car door to see what state the rest of him was in and decided that it would be too risky to try to ease him backwards into the driving seat before the paramedics ar-rived.

His car was just around the corner and with the keys that he'd been to retrieve still in his hand, he ran to get his bag, which was on the back seat.

It would be a poor comparison to what the ambulance would bring with it, but there were dressings and painkillers in it and various other items of basic first aid.

He'd seen Jemima supporting the girl as he'd run past.

She was sitting up, looking dazed and frightened with blood gushing from gashes to her legs.

His face had tightened. She'd probably had too much to drink and it had slowed down her reactions. Because of it she'd nearly got herself killed and an unsuspecting motorist had been seriously injured.

There was a surgical collar in the boot of his car which he'd intended dropping off to replace a soiled one that a patient had been using for some time, and he took it with him as he raced back to the scene. If he could stem the bleeding from the man's neck and ease the collar around it for support, he would at least be doing something useful, he thought.

Jemima was at his elbow the moment he got back, her face ashen in the light of the streetlamps. 'There was a nurse in the crowd,' she said, observing the tight contours of his face. 'I've left the girl with her for a moment. What can I do to help?'

He passed her a handful of antiseptic wadding.

'Try to stem the bleeding while I check that he's still breathing, and then we'll see if we can get a collar on him without moving his neck. Note the angle,' he pointed out grimly.

As they worked on the victim together Jemima thought wryly, So much for the enchanted evening. She'd walked out of the restaurant on cloud nine, only to fall off it into the middle of a street accident.

Within seconds the cavalry had arrived. Red-suited paramedics were spilling out of an ambulance, and the doctor with them was taking charge after a quick word with Jack.

When the injured had been taken to hospital, with lights flashing and sirens blaring, and the crowd had dispersed, Jack and Jemima went to get their cars. As they walked along the now deserted pavement Jemima said with a shudder, 'What a way to end the evening.'

His face was grim.

'Yes, indeed. We were caught up in the foolishness of others—alcohol over-indulgence on the girl's part and breaking the law on the driver's. Unfortunately there are still those who can't be bothered to fasten their seat belts, or think they're safer without them. We'll know another time to go far away from the madding crowd.'

'Like the top of Everest?'

He was smiling now.

'No way. They reckon it's busier up there than a town centre.'

When they reached the place where they'd parked the cars Jemima reached up and kissed him gently on the mouth.

'In spite of what's happened, it's been a lovely evening, Jack. Thank you for inviting me to share it with you.'

As his arms reached out for her she shook her head laughingly.

'What was it that you said about there being no doctors at the practice in the morning if we didn't get a move on? I'll see you tomorrow.' Without giving herself a chance to weaken, she unlocked the car door, started the engine and was gone.

CHAPTER SEVEN

THERE had been no requests for Jack's services on the lifeboat recently, and as long as the gallant craft was tucked away in the building at the top of the slipway, Jemima had put thoughts of what it stood for out of her mind.

The crew had been called out a couple of times to help vessels in distress, but on both occasions medical assistance hadn't been asked for.

With the onset of winter it was the coughs and colds season at the surgery, along with a variety of other ailments, and all three doctors were kept busy.

Jemima had been to have lunch with the mayoress on one of her days off and when she'd told Jack where she was going he'd said, 'I didn't know that the two of you were on such good terms. Some people think it's gone to her head, being mayoress. That she's living above her station.'

'You of all people should know not to judge a book by its cover...or a person by hearsay,' she'd chided.

'Point taken,' he'd replied. 'I suppose I asked for that.'

'With regard to Glenda,' she'd continued, 'she was left a large legacy by a friend, so why shouldn't she buy herself a nice house up there on the hill? It had nothing to do with her being mayoress. And as well as that...I like her. I always have. She gave me my first Saturday job, working in her Cornish cream shop.'

'All right!' he'd conceded. 'You've convinced me. Go and eat with your friend.'

*   *   *

'It's the mayoral ball soon,' Glenda told Jemima as they lunched in her elegant dining room. 'I've got two tickets for you if you'd like to go as my guest.'

Jemima looked at her in surprise.

'Really! I'd love to, but the question is…who with?'

'No man in your life, then?' the mayoress asked.

'Yes and no.'

'Tell me about it.'

'It's Jack Trelawney.'

Glenda clapped her hands.

'But of course! Who else could it be when you're working with the most attractive unattached man in Rockhaven?'

Jemima pulled a wry face. 'We're not exactly making much progress, though.'

'And why is that? You would be the perfect foil for his golden charm and vitality, with your glinting brown mane and pale skin.'

Jemima had to laugh.

'You make us sound like a couple out of one of the glossies, instead of two hardworking doctors who've both got hang-ups about certain things.'

'And what is it that's holding you back, Jemima?'

'Jack goes out with the lifeboat when medical assistance is required.'

'And very praiseworthy, too,' Glenda remarked. 'So what's the problem?'

'You know what happened to my father, Glenda. I couldn't go through that again.'

'Your dad wouldn't have wanted to die any other way,' her friend said gently. 'Obviously he wouldn't have wanted to die at all, but if it had to be, that's the way he'd have wanted to go…in the lifeboat service.'

'I know all that,' Jemima said raggedly, 'but I still feel the same about Jack's involvement.'

'Does he know?'

'Yes.'

'And has he offered to give it up?'

'No. And I can't ask it of him. I've been out there with them myself and I know what a vital service the lifeboats give.'

'And what are the hang-ups of the man in question that are putting the blight on the romance?'

'Women in general…and maybe a pushy ex-wife and her child.'

'Both of which are connected?'

'Yes, I suppose you could say that, but I also think that his mother wasn't exactly what she should have been either.'

'I don't know anything about that,' Glenda said, 'but I well remember Carla departing only days after they'd got back from their honeymoon. And when no information was forthcoming from the senior GP, most folks accepted the situation and left him to get on with it. But I do remember that he seemed to change overnight from an amiable practitioner to a brisk workaholic who kept his private affairs very close to his chest.'

'He still is like that,' Jemima had told her, and added with the vestige of a smile, 'but he does seem to be mellowing.'

'Since he met you?'

'Hmm. Possibly.'

'So hang in there,' Glenda had urged, 'and get the lifeboat situation into perspective.'

'I already have,' Jemima said with a shudder, and it seemed as if there was nothing else to say.

The tickets for the mayoral ball were still in her bag the week before it was to take place and Jemima knew that

there was only one person she wanted to take with her if
she went.

So why not ask him? she told herself. There could be no
harm in it. After all, he'd asked her out, and now it was
her turn to suggest they share a pleasant social occasion.
So she waylaid Jack one cold winter morning after surgery.

'I have two tickets for the mayoral ball which my friend
Glenda has given me,' she told him casually. 'Would you
be interested in joining me?'

As he stared at her in surprise Jemima thought that for
once she'd taken him unawares. It was nice to be in control
for a change.

'When is it?'

'Next Saturday.'

He was frowning.

'Am I to take it that you've asked everyone else and I'm
a last resort?'

Whew! she thought. Who was in charge now?

'No! Of course I haven't! Who would I know to ask,
anyway?'

'I'd have thought there were plenty of folk. After all, it
is your home town.'

She ignored the comment and told him with laboured
patience, 'I'm on the last minute with the invitation because
I thought you might not want to come.'

'And why would that be?'

'I don't know! Do I? But you are unpredictable.'

'I see.'

What was the matter with him? she wondered. Why
couldn't he just say yes or no? It seemed that he wasn't
going to say either.

'What time shall I pick you up?' he asked with brisk
sparcity of speech.

'Seven o'clock,' she told him with similar brevity and wished that she'd never mentioned the ball in the first place.

But on the night she was in a different frame of mind. The mayoral ball was Rockhaven's biggest social event of the Christmas season, and as anticipation rose in her Jemima thought that as things stood at present it might be her only outing, so she was going to make the most of it.

The dress that she'd bought specially for the occasion was of stiff black silk, decorated along the bodice and hem with gold beading.

It was the most sophisticated thing she'd ever chosen, with a full skirt and an off-the-shoulder neckline that showed off her youthful attractiveness to its full advantage.

For tonight she'd taken her hair off her face and it was swept back in long chestnut coils that fell against the milky whiteness of her shoulders. Her jewellery was of gold to match the decoration on the dress and the final effect was that of a smart sophisticate.

When she heard Jack's ring on the doorbell, panic took hold of her. She was gripped with an insane urge to rush into the bedroom and change into something that was more her, but there wasn't time. He was outside on the step and because she wasn't opening the door to him he was ringing the bell again.

Jack's expression when he saw her confirmed her worst fears. There was disappointment in it and as he stepped over the threshold he said, 'I thought you would be wearing the sea-nymph dress.'

Jemima was goggling at him. Sea nymph?

'The what?'

'The green silk.'

She swallowed and, looking down at the smart black gown, said, 'So you don't like this?'

'Yes, of course I do,' he said firmly. 'You look fantastic.

It's just that I've seen you in a green silk dress a couple of times and thought how it suited you.'

Her heart was leaping in her breast. She remembered wearing the green dress on her first night home when he'd found her on the headland, looking out to sea. Incredibly, after seeing her in it, he'd likened her to a beautiful sea creature. They hadn't been together five minutes and already her senses had been aroused.

'Let's go,' he said, as if the subject was closed. Taking her arm, he escorted her to his car.

Unable to stand for long, Glenda was seated on an ornate wooden chair to greet her guests, with the mayoral attendant standing respectfully beside her.

When she saw Jemima with the tall figure of Jack by her side, she smiled her pleasure.

They made a striking couple—the man with his amazing fairness and lithe grace, and the woman unusually elegant in black, with her beautiful hair swept back to enhance the fine-boned contours of her face.

Glenda saw that he had his hand beneath Jemima's elbow as they walked forward to greet her and that there was a restrained sort of protectiveness in his manner as he looked down at her.

What were they playing at, these two? Glenda wondered. She'd once dilly-dallied over a man that she'd loved, and someone else had been waiting in the wings, ready to step into the shoes that she'd hesitated to fill.

He was free. The immoral Carla was long gone out of his life. Or at least she should be. And Jemima had no ties with anyone else as far as she knew. Maybe tonight would give them a push in the right direction.

As the evening progressed Jemima was content. She'd

made this opportunity for them to be together again and was wondering how it would work out.

The food was delicious and when the meal was over the assembled gathering retired to where an orchestra was waiting to play for dancing.

As Jack took her in his arms and they moved smoothly along the ballroom floor, she thought that this was a fitting beginning to Christmas, whatever else it held.

His touch was warming her blood as it always did. His bright cobalt gaze, so close to hers, was telling her that she was desirable in spite of not having worn the green dress.

A patient collared Jack at one point in the evening, and while he was talking to the man Jemima went to have a word with Glenda.

'I've just been speaking to someone that you know,' the mayoress said. 'A young man from the Bristol area who's moving down here to open up a rest home. His uncle is on the council and I think he's going to assist with the finance.'

Jemima was eyeing her in surprise.

'Really? And he knows me? What's his name?'

'Mark Emmerson,' a voice said from behind her, and she whirled round to find the deputy clinical services manager from the Bristol hospital smiling at her.

As she reeled in dismayed astonishment Jemima's first thought was that if Mark had been hostile towards her when they'd parted, he seemed to have got over it as he was positively beaming.

'You look fantastic, Jemima,' he breathed. 'I only got here yesterday and was going to look you up the first chance I got…and here you are.'

He was hugging her to him and it was all she could do not to push him away. But he was an old friend and she

couldn't do that, so she kissed him on the cheek and sub-
mitted to the suffocating embrace.

Jack had finished chatting with his patient and was
watching them from across the dance floor. She could see
him over Mark's shoulder and hoped that he understood
what was happening.

'Let me introduce you to my partner for the evening,'
she said, quickly disentangling herself. Taking Mark's
hand, she led him towards where Jack was standing.

'This is Mark Emmerson, Jack,' she told him, trying to
sound cool. 'We worked at the same hospital in Bristol and
he's moving to the area.'

Feeling the need to explain, though she didn't know why,
as the two men shook hands she said, 'Jack is the senior
partner at the practice where I'm employed.'

As they made desultory small talk Jemima was contemplating having her ex-boyfriend living in Rockhaven. His
appearance had broken into the pleasure of the evening and
she hoped that he wasn't expecting them to take up where
they'd left off, as there'd been something just a bit too
clingy about that welcoming hug.

However, after a few moments he excused himself and
went to join his relations at the other side of the room. Her
spirits lifted, but they plummeted again as she began to
wonder why he'd not mentioned that he had folks in the
area before. He'd known where she came from and where
she was going back to. It was to be hoped that the move
hadn't been contrived.

'So how well do you know this fellow, Emmerson?' Jack
asked when he'd gone.

'We went out together for a while.'

'I see. And now?'

'Now...nothing.'

He smiled.

'So let's dance, Jemima Penrose.'

'Yes, please.' She beamed as her world righted itself.

Midnight had gone and the mayoress with it.

'I'm too tired to stay any longer,' she'd told Jemima, 'and my back's hurting. Enjoy yourself. I'll be in touch.'

It was half past one and the dance floor was filled with those up for the last dance. In a glow of pleasure Jemima was matching her steps to Jack's and putting all other thoughts to one side when the manager of the town hall came hurrying across to them.

'The emergency services have put a call out for all medical staff to report to the Chimes Hotel,' he said in a low voice. 'There's been a huge landslide and the building is about to fall into the sea. It hit the car park first and guests who were leaving after a similar event to this have been trapped in their cars, while those inside the building have been thrown about.'

They gazed at him speechlessly and Jemima thought, I don't believe this is happening. Not another evening with a blight on it!

'Right. We're on our way,' Jack was saying briskly, and as she lifted the long skirt of her dress to allow speed of movement, he took her arm and they left the ballroom at a run.

The Chimes Hotel was one of the biggest and most popular hotels in Rockhaven, but tonight it was in a sorry state. The cliff behind it had given way and tons of soil, sand and loose rock had come hurtling down onto the car park at the rear of the hotel.

Vehicles were piled on top of each other at strange angles, while others were buried up to roof height, and when the two doctors got there the fire brigade and ambulance services were already in action.

But much worse than that was what happened to the hotel. The force and weight of the landslide coming from behind had moved the building and now it was hanging over a drop to a rocky beach below.

Jack had taken in the scene with one brief glance and he said grimly, 'Do we attract catastrophes or do we not, Jemima?' He turned to the man in charge of the ambulance team. 'The surgery is only a couple of minutes away. I'll ring one of the staff on my mobile and ask them to open up, so that those not needing hospital treatment can be dealt with there.'

'Good idea,' the man said. 'We'll pass them along.'

'Where am I going to be of most use?' Jemima asked urgently.

The two men eyed the long back dress dubiously and Jack said, 'You're hardly dressed for it out here in the cold.'

He'd taken off his jacket and was rolling up the sleeves of his white evening shirt. Passing the jacket to her, he said, 'Here, put this on.'

Jemima was using her stole as a belt to hold the dress up and once she was huddled into his jacket she was ready for action.

The emergency services were frantically digging out the buried cars to check which of them had been occupied, all the time gazing anxiously at the overhanging cliff above them.

Jack was already bending over a man who had been dug out of one of them, bruised and bleeding, and a paramedic was attending to his wife nearby.

'Over there,' the ambulance man said, pointing to a colleague who was helping people to jump down from the tilting first floor of the hotel. 'There are still people inside there and some are badly injured.'

Jemima had gone almost before he'd finished speaking, and as Jack looked up briefly he saw a flash of gold evening shoes.

At last all the people were out of the building, some staggering down precarious staircases, others clawing their way along passages that had suddenly become steep, with the emergency services and anyone else who was available there to help them.

Jack had come to join Jemima and they were helping to assess them. Giving pain relief to those who needed it. Applying emergency dressings. Putting on collars for those with neck injuries. And all the time the loose cliff was hanging over them.

'I'm going to the surgery for more supplies,' he told her. 'We've nearly run out.' He touched her grimy cheek briefly. 'Watch what you're doing while I'm gone. It's none too safe around here.'

She nodded and went on with what she was doing.

An elderly woman in evening dress like herself was sitting nearby on the rubbish-strewn lawn of the hotel. She had a gash on her cheek, twigs in her hair and was in a dazed condition.

As Jemima looked at her, she got up and began to totter across to where the rescue services had just uncovered a silver Jaguar.

Jemima grabbed her arm. 'Don't go over there, madam,' she cried urgently, but the woman shrugged off her restraining arm and surged forward again.

At that moment the cry went up, 'Look out! It's on the move again!'

All those working on the parked cars ran towards the road that lay beside the hotel, but even if she understood what was going on, the woman wasn't quick enough and Jemima couldn't leave her.

As she grasped the arm that was hanging limply by the woman's side the new slide came, a shuddering of sticks, stones and tree roots moving so fast that there was no time to get out of the way. Pushing the woman to the ground, Jemima threw herself on top of her.

When the first stone hit her Jemima thought illogically that Jack would wonder where she was when he came back.

Then survival took over her mind as she braced herself for what was to come. As the avalanche thundered towards them she wondered if she would ever see him again. She could hear someone calling his name, but in her distress didn't recognise the voice as her own.

Jack had got Helen out of bed and she was at the surgery almost as soon as the first casualties began to arrive.

One of the practice nurses had been going past on the way home from a party of her own. When she'd seen the lights on she'd gone inside to investigate and was now also assisting.

He was relieved to find everything under control and was about to depart with the fresh supplies when a paramedic came in with a couple who'd been hurt by flying glass.

'There's been another slide and one of the doctors is trapped beneath it,' the fellow said.

A stillness had fallen on the room and the ambulance crewman said uncomfortably, 'She'd been to some sort of gathering herself. She was wearing a long black dress with a man's dinner jacket over it.'

Jack's face had gone grey and Helen said anxiously, 'It's not Jemima, is it?'

There was no answer. Jack had gone. Into the dark night with fear as his companion.

As he sped over the distance between the practice and the hotel Jack was tearing away the rubble in his mind's eye, flinging it to one side with frenzied desperation. But supposing that Jemima was already dead...

When he got there he saw that the earth had settled again and the rescue operations were once more under way. But where was Jemima?

'Dr Penrose...where is she?' he asked frantically of the nearest member of a group of firemen.

The man lifted a grimy face from his task of digging around a car that was just becoming visible. He pointed to the other side of the car park where a new pile of rubble was being attacked by others like him.

'Under there,' he said briefly. 'The Doc went after a woman who was in the path of the last slide and couldn't get her away fast enough.' A shout had just gone up and he found himself talking to Jack's fast departing back.

'We've got 'em! They're here, under the branches of a tree,' someone cried as Jack was flinging himself across the car park.

The dread inside him was like nothing he'd ever known as he pushed his way through to the front. It felt as if his blood had turned to ice and his heart had stopped beating. Death was part of the job for any doctor. He accepted that. But not this way, he thought frantically. Not now. Not Jemima!

Amazingly it was the branches rather than the trunk of the tree that were over the two women and the sturdy boughs had provided a degree of shelter which had saved their lives.

They were both dazed but miraculously they were alive, and as his body went slack with relief Jack said urgently, 'Oxygen first before we move them, and then let's get them away from here before any more comes down. But I want to check for broken bones and spinal injuries first. There are a lot of people now in wheelchairs who weren't checked over before they were moved after an accident.' And that wasn't going to happen to his sea nymph. Not if he could help it.

On the way to hospital some time later Jemima held Jack's hand tightly. She felt dreadful. Her back and shoulders were hurting from where she'd taken the onslaught of the avalanche before the branches had provided their merciful cover and that, along with multiple cuts and bruises, was creating a state of general agony.

The fact that Jack had been the first person she'd seen when the tree had been lifted off them had brought tears to her eyes. She'd thought he'd been at the surgery, supervising things there, but he must have heard that voice that was calling for him, she thought groggily.

'You've hurt your spine,' he'd told her after examining her with deft fingers, adding as they'd carried her carefully to the ambulance, 'But as you can move your legs I'm hoping that the damage to the vertebrae isn't too serious.'

'Where's the lady I was with?' Jemima croaked. 'And who was in the silver Jaguar?'

'She has minor injuries and is being put in an ambulance at this moment,' Jack told her. 'It was her husband in the car. He saw the landslide coming, knew he hadn't time to get out, so wisely made sure that all the doors and windows were shut. The vehicle is badly damaged but he escaped unhurt. Which is more than one can say about others in the car park and in the hotel, with furniture sliding all over the place and partition walls coming down as the building moved.'

His face was grim. 'Thankfully there have been no fatalities so far.'

He dredged up a smile. 'You did a great job of saving her life. There were moments when I wasn't too sure how it would turn out,' he said sombrely as his hold on her hand tightened. 'But I told the fates that they had to keep you safe. That it wasn't the time for you to go…and I wasn't going to allow it. The last time they dished out the dirt I accepted it, but not now.'

The tears were threatening again. It sounded as if he cared…a lot…but it wasn't the time for mind-searching. Managing a smile of her own, Jemima joked, 'Don't mention dirt. I feel as if I've swallowed a sackful.'

As the ambulance screeched to halt outside the hospital Jemima said weakly, 'What about the practice? Supposing they keep me in.'

'Forget the practice,' Jack said tersely. 'Finding out what damage you've suffered is the main priority at this moment.'

X-rays showed that the vertebrae at the bottom of Jemima's spine were thankfully not broken, but they were cracked and would have to heal of their own accord. But Jemima's clavicle *was* broken, which meant keeping her arm in a sling until that also had healed.

'I'd like to keep you in for a couple of days,' the consultant in Accident and Emergency said. 'After that, is there anyone to look after you until you feel better? There's a lot of bruising and grazes that are going to give some discomfort, as well as the after effects of shock.'

'No. I live alone,' she told him, 'but I'll survive.'

She watched Jack open his mouth to speak, but forestalled him. With a conciliatory smile for both men she said, 'I *am* a doctor and I'll take care of myself.'

When the consultant had gone Jack stood looking down at her in the small cubicle where they had put her until a bed was vacant.

'I was going to suggest that you come to my place when

they discharge you from here. You knew that, didn't you, Jemima? So why be so quick to say you can manage?'

'Because I can,' she said wearily.

It didn't seem the moment to explain that she didn't want to be in the way if Carla and the little boy were going to be with him in the days to come. If there was any unfinished business between them, she didn't want to be an onlooker.

'All right. We'll discuss it another time. It's almost daybreak,' he said evenly, adding with an anxious frown, 'You're exhausted, and no wonder with what you've gone through. It seems like a lifetime since we were at the Mayor's Ball.'

Jemima nodded mutely. He was right. They'd been transferred from paradise to hell in a matter of minutes and those were two reasons why she would never forget this night.

A nurse was hovering.

'We're ready to transfer you to the ward, Dr Penrose,' she said. 'Doctor has ordered a sedative so…'

'You'd like me to go?' Jack said wryly.

'If you don't mind.'

He bent and his lips touched her brow briefly.

'I'll be back later. Goodbye, Jemima…and don't worry about a thing.'

She nodded meekly. It was all she could do under the circumstances, but what she really wanted was for him to stay, to hold her, to be there every time she dreamt that there was a wall of rock and soil hurtling down on her…and to tell her that he loved her.

Maybe he would have done if they hadn't become involved in the tragedy at the Chimes Hotel.

The sedative was beginning to take effect and Jemima was in a relaxed state when the same nurse appeared beside her in the ward to say that she had a visitor.

'I wouldn't normally let him in at this hour,' she said, 'but in view of what happened up there on the cliffs and the fact that he's very concerned, I'm going to turn a blind eye, but only for a few minutes.'

'Who is it?' Jemima asked drowsily.

'It's me. Mark,' a familiar voice said.

That brought her awake.

'Mark! What are you doing here?'

'My folks and I had left the ball before you, so we knew nothing about the landslide until my uncle got a phone call at six o'clock this morning to say that an urgent council meeting has been arranged for nine o'clock. It was then that I heard what had happened to you.'

'Yes, I see.'

It was good of him to come, she was thinking, but Mark was the last person she felt like talking to. The only man she wanted had gone.

'Can I get you anything?' he asked.

Jemima shook her head. He really was kind but she was tired and... She raised a weary hand to her brow and her glance rested on the sleeve of the winceyette nightdress they'd found for her.

'You could go to my house and collect me some things,' she told him impulsively. 'Nightwear, a robe, toiletries, slippers, and anything else you think I'll need for a couple of days or more.'

She really was fighting sleep now and her voice was thick and slurred as she explained, 'My evening bag is in the locker and the keys to my cottage are in it.'

When he left the hospital Jack went straight to the practice. He hadn't been in touch since the moment he'd heard what had happened to Jemima.

That item of news had wiped out every other thought

from his mind, but now he was back in focus, having been totally put out at her refusal to let him take care of her.

Surely she wasn't still on the defensive about the lifeboat business, he thought as he left the hospital in a cold dawn. What if she was? It was her well-being they were talking about.

Yes, the voice of reason agreed…her physical well-being. But maybe Jemima was more concerned with her mental well-being.

Helen and the practice nurse were clearing up when he got there, having treated all those who had needed on-the-spot first aid, and now the place was empty.

They were both desperate to know about Jemima and relieved to know that it wasn't as bad as they'd expected.

'Do we know what the situation is at the hotel?' he asked. 'Is it still on the edge?'

'Yes, as far as we know,' Helen told him. 'The council is having an urgent meeting first thing this morning.'

He was dreading asking. 'And the casualties?'

'Some badly injured,' she said sombrely, 'but no fatalities.'

'A grim Christmas for some, then,' he remarked.

He wasn't looking forward to his own with the Carla problem on his doorstep, but that was nothing compared to this.

'I'm going home to get showered and changed and then I'm heading back to the hospital,' he told them. 'Bethany has gone away for the weekend and it looks as if she's going to be coming back to a staff shortage.'

CHAPTER EIGHT

FOR once there was no feeling of relaxation as Jack stood beneath the warm spray of the shower. He was too tense. Only hours ago he had thought that he was going to find Jemima either dead or horribly injured, and it had made him understand how she felt about the lifeboat.

Her descent into danger hadn't been her own choice. *His* was. He ought to remove that shadow from her mind and ask to be relieved from lifeboat duty. It was against all his inclinations, but it wasn't every doctor who went out with them that had a woman in his life who'd watched her father die as the Severn had battled through a horrendous storm. So he owed her that.

As he towelled himself dry he was deciding what he was going to do next. First a quick breakfast and then a trip to the cottage to collect some clothes for her. He still had a key that Hazel had once given him and was relieved that he hadn't passed it back to Jemima. To have her own things around her would make her feel better.

But he had a strong feeling that today she was going to be feeling pretty grim with plenty of aches and pains, not the least being a very sore back.

When he got to the cottage he paused in the porch. The door was ajar. His nerve ends tightened. Burglars were all Jemima needed, and he marched inside with his anger rising. But he was stopped in his tracks when a figure appeared at the top of the stairs and the fellow they'd met the night before called down to him.

'What are *you* doing here?' Jack asked in cold surprise as he began to mount the staircase.

'Jemima asked me to pack her some things,' Mark said. 'I called in at the hospital as soon as I heard what had happened.'

'I see. And what time was that?' Jack enquired tightly as he observed the lingerie and other clothes laid out on her bed.

'An hour ago.'

'And did she give you permission to root amongst her personal possessions?'

If the other man felt the chill he gave no sign. He merely smiled and said, 'You mean the skimpies? I've seen them all before.'

'Have you really? Then in that case you'd better get on and deliver them, hadn't you?'

'Sure thing,' Mark agreed smugly. 'Any message for her?'

'No!' Jack said through gritted teeth, 'but I've got one for you. Cause Jemima any hassle and you'll have me to deal with.'

'Yes, Doctor,' Mark said coolly, and, throwing the clothes into a small holdall, he went.

When he'd gone Jack sank down on to the bed disconsolately. So much for his own big ideas, he thought. How could she ask that smoothie to rummage in the drawers in her bedroom?

There'd been no signs of anything between them last night at the ball, but she'd admitted that they'd gone out together in Bristol, and if what the smarm had just said was true, it had gone a bit further than that. Maybe her being injured had resulted in a fresh surge of feeling between them.

Ugh! He couldn't bear the thought of it! And he'd been

contemplating letting down the lifeboat service for a woman who had another man in her life.

When Mark appeared at her bedside in the middle of the morning Jemima stifled a groan. She needed the night-clothes he'd brought, but she needed Jack more.

Where was he? She felt terrible. As if every bone in her body ached. She needed the sight of him to make her feel better.

'Have you seen Jack?' she asked weakly as Mark deposited the bag beside her bed.

'No,' he told her blandly, 'but I suppose he might be catching up on his sleep after being up all night.'

'Yes, I suppose so,' she agreed, turning her face into the pillow.

'I'm here for you, though,' he said coaxingly. 'I've missed you since you left Bristol, Jemima. That's why I decided to move to this part of the world.'

Her spirits sank. So it wasn't just by accident that Mark was in Rockhaven. The sooner he was made to realise that what she'd said in Bristol still applied, the better. Yet she didn't want to hurt him. He was a decent guy in his own way, although next to Jack he was nothing.

She sighed. The last thing she felt like doing in her present state was telling him that nothing had changed, that she wasn't interested in him as anything other than a friend. But do it she must, otherwise he might get all sorts of ideas in his head.

'It's good of you to be concerned about me, Mark,' she told him with a placatory smile, 'but, please, don't get any ideas about us carrying on where we left off in Bristol. As far as I'm concerned, it's over between us.'

A nurse appearing at that moment was her salvation. 'Dr Penrose is due to be seen by one of the consultants any moment, sir,' she said to Mark, 'and then she must rest. If you want to visit again, later in the day would be a better time.'

Mark was already on his feet and there was defeat in the set of his mouth.

'OK, Jemima, I get the message,' he said. 'It's Trelawney, isn't it?' And before she could either confirm or deny it he'd gone.

'So, your friend Mark has delivered the goods, I see,' Jack said when he saw the case beside the bed on his arrival shortly afterwards.

'Er…yes. How did you know?'

'I went round to the cottage to do the very same thing but he'd got there before me,' he told her tonelessly as his concerned glance took in the discoloration of her face and arms.

Jemima looked at him anxiously. If she tried to explain why she'd asked Mark to bring her some clothes he might wonder why she felt she had to mention it—and if she didn't he might think she was being secretive. Better to do neither, she decided…and talk about something else.

'What's sent him scuttling off?' he asked before she'd had the chance to do so.

'The nurse. The consultant is coming to see me any moment.'

'Right,' Jack said decisively. 'I'm staying until he's been. I want a word with him once he's examined you and then I'll go, as I don't think you're in any fit state for company—not mine, anyway—and I do have other things to do.'

So much for that, she thought dismally. He had slotted her into his busy day and would soon be off. Couldn't he see that, bruised and battered as she was, she wanted him to hold her, comfort her, tell her he cared?

She supposed he did care…up to a point. Inasmuch as he'd come to check up on her in the role of her GP. No doubt, last night's magic had been filed away in that orderly mind of his and today was another day. Well, two could play at that game.

'By all means, don't let me being in here interrupt your busy day,' she told him, determined not to let him see how she was hurting.

At that moment the man in charge appeared with his entourage tagging on behind, and Jack went to check up on some of their practice members in another ward who had been admitted after the previous night's harrowing incident.

When he went back to her, Jemima was sitting up in bed, gazing desolately into space. The sight of her made him determined not to upset her further with any comments about the man who'd appeared out of the blue the night before.

That they were closer than he'd thought was quite obvious, and it pained him to think that she hadn't made it clear earlier. But that was the name of the game where he and the opposite sex were concerned. He was a fool to have expected any different.

Yet his voice was gentle as he asked, 'What did the consultant have to say?'

She managed a smile.

'Not a lot. He's satisfied that my back is going to be all right and has checked me over to make sure there's nothing else they haven't picked up on. Then he recommended a few days' rest to get me on the mend.'

'Good,' he said soberly. 'You could have been killed!'

'Yes, I know. But I wasn't, was I? And neither was the other lady.'

'Thanks to you.'

'I suppose so,' she agreed flatly, being in no mood for medals. She'd already had the woman's grateful husband expressing his thanks and was hoping that would be the end of it.

Last night there had been a magical bond between Jack and herself. They had spun a blissful web around themselves. But today he was coldly polite. Caring, yes, but in a doctor-patient sort of way that was making her heart ache.

She didn't know why he was acting like he was. He was concerned but aloof, and if it was because of Mark he obviously hadn't believed her when she'd said it was over.

'I have things to do, Jemima,' he was saying levelly. 'If you need anything, get in touch.'

'Yes. Thank you,' she said weakly, and watched him go with a heavy heart.

Jemima was sleeping the sleep of someone wanting to shut out the present and not too keen to face up to the future when a nurse awakened her in the late evening.

'Dr Trelawney phoned to ask how you are,' she said. 'He apologised for ringing so late but apparently he's been settling in some visitors at his place. His ex-wife and her son, I believe.'

As Jemima's spirits hit rock bottom she went on, 'He also asked me to tell you that he's tried to get in touch with your mother to let her know what has happened, but he says that she appears to be away from home.'

Jemima sank back against the pillows. The fact that Jack hadn't been able to contact her mother was a relief. Hazel didn't react well to any kind of injury or illness.

As for the rest of the message, what had she been expecting? A call to say he was missing her and would be in to see her again the moment he got the chance? That every second they were apart was like a lifetime?

No. He'd wanted her to know that he'd offered his home to Carla and little Callum. A kind and generous thing to do under the circumstances. So why did she feel like banging her fists against the wall?

If Jack had been feeling depressed before, the arrival of another man's child on his doorstep in the charge of his ex-wife didn't do anything to make him feel better.

The last time they'd discussed them moving in with him he'd told Carla, 'I must be insane to be even contemplating it, and if the need for somewhere to stay just applied to you, Carla, the answer would be a definite no. But I can't stomach the idea of that little boy being incarcerated in the dismal bed and breakfast place where you're staying, so I suppose I'm going to say yes. You can stay with me until Derrick comes out of hospital. But it's on one condition.'

'And what's that?' she'd asked with a triumphant smile.

'That you sort out your life. If your partner is ill you should be with him. You haven't said what's wrong with him and I don't particularly want to know. I just hope that he's soon better…and that you're telling the truth when you say he's sick. That this isn't just a ploy to get us back together, because there's no chance of that whatsoever.

'If I take you both into my place, the moment Derrick is fit to talk you start trying to make a go of it—for Callum's sake if no one else's. Do you get the message?'

She'd rolled her eyes heavenwards and shrugged narrow shoulders, but he'd known that she'd finally accepted that she didn't figure in any of his future plans. And today, of all days, they'd appeared, when his mind was full of Jemima and the man from her past.

Little Callum had been tired and fretful after the long journey from Scotland and after he'd been fed he'd fallen fast asleep.

His face had been grimy when he'd arrived, so had his clothes, and his hair needed cutting, which made Jack decide that come Monday morning he would insist that Carla take him to the toddlers' clinic at the surgery.

He stood looking down on him as he slept and knew that the bitterness he'd carried around for so long had gone. Carla would always be what she was, feckless and faithless, but as for the defenceless little boy, *he* had done him no wrong.

The boy wakened during the night and began to cry when he saw that he was in a strange place. When there was no sign of Carla, who had been helping herself to the contents of his wine cabinet, Jack took the child into the kitchen and gave him a drink of milk then took him into his own bed and cuddled him until he slept again.

Would he ever have a child of his own? he wondered sombrely as he looked down at the flushed little face beneath its unkempt locks.

Not from the way things were going. Of late he'd dared to imagine what kind of a child he and Jemima would have, and his loins had ached with longing at the thought, but once again his judgement appeared to be at fault.

Docile for once, Carla had agreed to take Callum to the practice, and when Jack left to take surgery the next morning she was bathing him and changing him into clean clothes that they'd brought with them.

His face had been grim as he'd watched her. How could she just take off and leave her child? he'd thought, but there was obviously more to what was going on than she was prepared to say.

Before he started his house calls Jack went to the hospital

to see Jemima. He was praying that the Emmerson fellow wouldn't be there but had decided that, whether he found himself as an unwelcome presence or not, he had to see her.

He needn't have worried. Neither of them were visible and a smiling nurse told him, 'Dr Penrose has been discharged. The consultant saw her this morning and said she could go home.'

Jack's sigh had frustration in it. Jemima had gone home and hadn't let him know, so obviously he wasn't needed.

'Did someone come for her?' he asked casually.

'I don't know,' was the reply. 'I was with another patient at the time.'

'Yes, of course,' he said, and went to check on the other casualties from the hotel incident.

They had all been discharged except for an elderly man who'd had a heart attack when the hotel had begun to slide and a young waitress with a badly fractured leg.

There were others still being treated but they weren't his patients, and as Jack drove back to the practice the memory of those awful moments when Jemima had been buried beneath the debris came back.

When he'd bent over her after they'd lifted the tree off them, the look on her face had made him think she cared for him…loved him even…but that idea had been short-lived, and now she'd gone home without even telling him. No doubt, with lover boy falling over himself to hold her hand.

When the taxi had dropped her off outside the cottage Jemima took a deep breath. There had been moments on Saturday night when she'd thought she might not see it again. But the fates had been kind and now, as she unlocked the door with her free hand, she was facing up to another situation that had dread in it.

When Jack had said that he'd had lots to do yesterday and had made a quick exit, she'd only discovered late in the evening that Carla was now *in situ* and, whether he still had feelings for his ex-wife or not, she'd decided there was no way that she was going to break into the threesome by asking him to bring her home.

Instead of being a comfort to her when she'd needed him after the accident, he'd been offhand and prickly. For what reason she didn't know. But it had occurred to her that he was perhaps seeing their relationship in the light of extra baggage now that he'd committed himself to housing Carla and her child.

Mark hadn't been near since their talk the previous day, and if he turned up at the hospital to pressure her further, he would be someone else who would find her gone.

As the day progressed she realised that she wasn't as pain-free as she'd thought she would be, and in the middle of the afternoon she went upstairs to rest.

A glorious winter sunset drew her to the window and as she looked out onto the headland she saw them. A family group. Man, woman and child, Jack, Carla and the little Callum, who was throwing a ball and gurgling with excitement every time they threw it back to him.

They *weren't* a family, of course. Only the woman and the boy were related. Somewhere he already had a father. But it still made Jemima's desolation increase because she was on the outside of Jack's life looking in. He'd made time to walk with them before the early evening surgery and she knew herself to be envious.

At half past seven her doorbell rang, and when she opened the door Jack was on the step.

'Well?' he questioned briefly as she stepped back to let him over the threshold.

'Well...what?'

'How are you? How are you coping with only one free arm?'

She managed a pale smile. 'As well as can be expected...to quote a well-used phrase in the N.H.S.'

'How did you get home?'

'By taxi.'

'So Emmerson didn't bring you?'

'No.'

'Why didn't you ring me?'

'Because you were busy.'

'Not that busy!'

'Have your visitors settled in?'

'Yes, it would seem so,' he said irritably. 'But we were talking about you, Jemima. Are you going to be able to wash and dress yourself and make a meal?'

'Of course,' she said confidently. 'Remember, my hand is free. It's more my elbow and shoulder that are restricted.'

He was frowning.

'I'm surprised Mark hasn't moved in to look after you. He was fussing around enough at the hospital.'

'How many times do I have to tell you that I can manage?' she snapped, angered that he was trying to fob her off onto Mark. She noticed that *he* wasn't volunteering but, then, he couldn't, could he?

'All right,' he growled. 'No need to flip your lid, but I'll be keeping an eye on you whether you like it or not.'

'I'm intending to turn up for surgery as soon as I can,' she told him coolly. 'Who's dealing with my patients?'

'Bethany and I between us.'

'And the hotel? *Has* it fallen into the sea?'

'Not as yet. It's been shored up until tomorrow when a demolition firm is moving in.'

Surely now he would mention the ball, Jemima thought desperately in the pause that followed, but he was turning to go as if holding her close in that beautiful ballroom had meant nothing.

She decided to jog his memory.

'It was a shame that Glenda's ball was cut short, wasn't it?'

His face tightened.

'Yes, too bad, but the interruption did come during the last waltz...if you remember...and after you'd renewed your acquaintance with a past lover.'

'And what is that supposed to mean?'

He sighed as if she were some wearisome child. 'I would have thought there was no need to ask.'

His hand was on the doorknob and she wanted to pull him back, but his next words made her realise that Jack had other things on his mind.

'I'm concerned about Callum,' he said tersely. 'He's spent a lot of time being passed around between friends and acquaintances since Carla left, as his father has had to go to work. He looked a bit uncared for when they arrived, though he was perking up when we walked along the headland this afternoon. But I shall be watching him keenly. I insisted that Carla take him to the toddlers' clinic at the surgery this morning, and the nurses gave him a thorough examination.'

'And?'

'They said he was in good health but somewhat disorientated after being moved from pillar to post over the last few weeks.'

'Well, he would be, wouldn't he?' Jemima said. 'I would

never leave a child of mine, no matter what was going on in my life.'

Jack didn't agree or disagree. Instead, he said, 'Carla is like a child herself…a spoilt one, as Derrick Draycott will have discovered. Still, there's a child involved. He has to be protected.'

As Jack opened the door and went striding towards the gate, a blast of cold air came in from the sea and Jemima thought that its chill was nothing compared to the coldness around her heart.

What was the matter with him? she asked herself again. He'd sounded as if he was about to make some ridiculous commitment to Carla because of the boy. The child already had a father, for heaven's sake! And whatever he was like, at least *he* hadn't deserted his son.

Waiting until she knew Jack would be out on his morning calls, Jemima rang the surgery on Tuesday and told Bethany that she would be in the following day.

'Are you sure that you're well enough?' the gentle doctor asked, and Jemima smiled on the other end of the line.

'Yes,' she assured her. 'My aches and pains are wearing off and the sling isn't too much of an inconvenience. The only thing is, I'll be on foot as I won't be able to drive. But I'll be able to do all the nearby house calls that don't require a car.'

'We've missed you, Jemima,' the other woman said. 'Jack has been irritable and edgy and that ex-wife of his is calling in all the time. The child is a sweet little poppet, though. Jack adores kids and seems really taken with him.'

When she'd put the phone down Jemima slumped onto the nearest chair. If she'd been low-spirited before, the chat with Bethany had made her feel a thousand times worse.

If Jack could love a child belonging to the faithless

woman he'd once been married to, he was to be admired. But it seemed as if his tolerance didn't extend to herself, and the injustice of it was that she didn't know what she'd done.

Surely Mark appearing from the past wasn't the cause of his frostiness. Admittedly, Mark had been at pains to make his presence felt at the hospital and unfortunately was going to be a permanent fixture in Rockhaven from now on, but he'd had no encouragement from her and wasn't likely to be getting any.

Suddenly she was on her feet, her apathy gone. If Jack couldn't cope with a man friend from the past showing her some concern and affection, he could get lost! And if he wanted to start sniffing around his ex, he could get on with it. She would show him if she cared!

The first thing Jemima saw the next morning was that Jack's four-wheel-drive wasn't outside the practice.

The second thing that took her eye was the large Christmas tree in the waiting room and the corridors and reception area bright with tinsel and holly.

Her heart sank. In the last few days the festive season had been the last thing on her mind. The events of Saturday night had blotted out all thoughts of it, but now she was facing the reality that Christmas was only a short time away, and she wished it wasn't.

There had been no word from her mother and James, so she'd realised that they must still be away and that she would have to wait until they came back before finding out if they would be coming to Cornwall for Christmas.

She had mixed feelings about it. It would be nice to see them both. To have some company might lift her spirits as, with Jack having a full house, they would have to stay at Surf Cottage.

But there would almost certainly be family gatherings at some time over the holiday, and did she want to have to pretend that all was well between them when they were all together?

An even more painful thought was that he wouldn't want to leave Carla and Callum behind if he came...not at Christmas.

Hope spiralled weakly inside her that by then Jack's ex-wife might have gone. And supposing she had? What difference would it make if he still intended keeping Jemima herself out in the cold?

She'd noticed that the lifeboat was out as she'd walked along the seafront to the surgery, and the fact that Jack's car wasn't there made her wonder if there was a connection.

Fear clutched at her heart. The sight of the big doors wide open and the empty building behind them was something she could do without.

It was a cold blustery morning, with the Atlantic breakers grey and angry as they came bounding in, and she shuddered. But Bethany was able to calm her anxieties.

'Jack is going to be late in this morning,' she said. 'He's not on board the Severn if that's what you're thinking.'

'I was, as a matter of fact,' Jemima admitted. 'I can't explain what it does to me when I see the lifeboat, and it's even worse when I see the empty boathouse. I never used to be like that. Going out when I was needed was a way of life I'd grown up with, but after my dad was drowned it changed, and I can't face the thought of it and what it stands for. But enough of my fears and foibles. There's nothing wrong with Jack, is there?'

'No, not with him. But there's a problem with the child's father. You know he's in hospital somewhere in Scotland, having major heart surgery?'

'I knew he was in hospital but didn't know what for.'

'Right, well, that's it—a triple bypass which was carried out successfully on Monday, but yesterday he had a relapse. Some sort of infection he picked up. He's now seriously ill.'

'And she left him to face that on his own,' Jemima breathed. 'What sort of a woman is she?'

Bethany smiled. 'Maybe not as bad as we think. The seriousness of his condition has brought her up with a jolt and she was frantic when she heard what had happened. Carla left for Scotland on the first train this morning and Jack is trying to get Callum into a nursery for a few days until she comes back.'

'And in the meantime he's going to look after him?' Jemima asked.

'Yes, it would appear so.'

'That will be no easy task with the practice to see to.'

'No, it won't, but hopefully it won't be for long.'

And what if Callum's father dies? Jemima thought as she went into her own sanctum. Callum and Carla would be a one-parent family, and she'd already shown that she didn't care all that much about Derrick. What would Jack do then? Take them permanently under his wing?

A young mother with a beautiful baby girl was one of her patients during the morning. It was clear to see that she was a cherished child, lovingly clothed and cared for, and Jemima couldn't help remembering what Jack had said about Callum.

Parents were all the luck of the draw, she thought with Carla and Hazel in mind, and as she smiled reassuringly at the worried mother she could tell that this child was a winner.

'Davina is teething, Doctor,' the mother said with her

voice rising anxiously, 'and as well as not sleeping at night, she's become very chesty since yesterday.'

The baby had a spot of bright red colour on each cheek and when Jemima sounded her chest she was croaky. But when she gently held the infant's tongue down with a spatula, it showed that there was no inflammation of the throat and that her first two teeth were almost through.

'What have you been giving her?' Jemima asked.

'Calpol.'

'Good. Keep on with it. Davina *is* a bit chesty but the teeth should be through any time and once they arrive the other problems will clear...that is, until the next tooth, or teeth, start pushing their way through.'

When they had gone, with the little miss howling lustily at having her tender mouth interfered with, Jemima sat back in her chair and let her thoughts turn to what Bethany had said.

The least she could do was to offer to help Jack with Callum, and if he wouldn't accept it, she really would know that the relationship that had barely taken root was over.

CHAPTER NINE

'So is it sorted?' Jemima asked when Jack arrived in the late morning looking less than his usual cool self.

He frowned. 'I see that Bethany's been filling you in.'

'Yes.'

'So you'll be aware that Draycott is on the critical list?'

'Er…yes. That's bad news for everyone, isn't it? I believe that Carla has gone to be with him and that you've been trying to register Callum with a nursery.'

'Correct on all counts,' he said flatly. 'So what's the situation here? Who took my surgery?'

'We did it between us.'

He was moving towards his consulting room but he stopped in his tracks when she said, 'You didn't answer my question. Have you managed to place Callum?'

'Yes. I'll take him each morning while Carla is away and pick him up after the early evening surgery.'

'That's a long time for a child to be with strangers.'

He sighed.

'Maybe. But what else can I do?'

'Nothing. You're doing enough already. I was about to say that I'd be pleased to help if there's anything I can do.'

He was observing her in surprise and she wondered why. Did the man in her life think she was too wrapped up in her own affairs, such as they were, to care about him and the boy?

It seemed as if it might be so.

'I'd have thought that you'd be wanting to spend any free time you have with Emmerson.'

If there'd been surprise in Jack's eyes, now there was anger in hers.

'Well, you thought wrong! Why do you keep harping on about Mark? I know he was hovering around when I was in hospital, but that was out of concern.'

'Oh, yes? I found him in your house, rummaging amongst your clothes...with your permission, of course.'

Jemima looked at him blankly.

'That's right. I forgot to ask you to pack me a bag and Mark appeared just after you left.'

It was on the tip of his tongue to tell her that he'd been mad with jealousy ever since the other man had come out with the smug inference that had made him think they'd slept together, and that he was grateful for the trauma he was involved in on his ex-wife's behalf as it was taking his mind off another close encounter with the unreliable sex.

'So, *are* you going to let me help you with Callum?' she persisted, determined to change what was becoming an increasingly provoking subject.

'What did you have in mind?'

'Washing his clothes. Making the evening meal for the three of us, so that you don't have to start after you've been to pick him up. If you can manage without me at evening surgery, you could collect him when you've finished your afternoon calls then I could feed Callum at a sensible time for a toddler and have him tucked up in bed by the time you've finished at the practice.'

'You'd have to come round to my place to do all that.'

'So? What's the problem?'

'None,' he admitted stiffly, 'if you're happy to do it.'

Jemima wanted to shake him, tell him that he was blind if he couldn't see that she would do anything to help give him peace of mind.

But for some reason he was as prickly as a hedgehog

and even though Mark had been to the fore of late she'd already told Jack that their relationship was part of the lack-lustre past.

Maybe she hadn't made it clear enough, and with that thought in mind she stepped up to him and kissed him gently on the mouth.

Jemima felt him tense, but he didn't respond. Undeterred, she murmured, 'How could I mind doing something for a little one whose parents aren't there to care for him, and for a man who covers up the fact that he has a heart by surrounding himself with protective armour?'

'And why do you think that is?' he said through gritted teeth as his hands came out to grip her forearms. 'It's because this…' His mouth was claiming hers now and it wasn't gentle. He lifted his head. 'And this…' he kissed her again '…are entrapments for the gullible male.'

That did it! Jemima heaved him away as if he had something catching.

'Gullible!' she cried. 'You! Gullible! Crazy would be a better word. There's torment in you that's clouding your judgement. I thought that you'd changed your mind about me. Tom has a lot to answer for,' she went on angrily. 'I always thought that it was women who were malicious, but he was in a class of his own…and so are you, Jack.'

'How do you expect me to feel?' he slammed back. 'Emmerson was handling your underwear as if it was as familiar to him as his own Y-fronts.'

'What?'

'Yes, and if I'd had any doubts, he made sure I knew he'd seen it all before. And there I was on the point of resigning from my lifeboat commitments because I didn't want to cause you any distress.'

Jemima was listening, open-mouthed.

'The only time Mark ever saw me undressed was one

night when he came barging into the locker room when I was changing out of my hospital clothes,' she gasped. 'I don't know why I should feel the need to justify myself, but for your information I'm one of that group of untrendy women who—'

'Untrendy?' he butted in disbelievingly.

Jemima ignored the interruption.

'I'm a virgin, Jack.'

She watched him try to swallow, as if his neck muscles had gone into paralysis, but there was no triumph in her. Just a great sadness. He hadn't trusted her. He'd doubted her at the beginning and nothing had changed. There was just one more thing to say.

'And with regard to the lifeboat, don't ever think of denying those sick and in peril because of me. Even if I'm letting them down, there's no call for you to do so...and in spite of your poor opinion of me, my offer of help still stands.'

On that pronouncement she went to start her morning calls. As Jack made no attempt to stop her, Jemima concluded that the barriers were still up.

That assumption lasted until the middle of the afternoon when she opened the door of the cottage and found him on the step with his small charge in his arms.

'I've done as you suggested,' he said as she stepped back to let them in.

'What? Taken stock of the way you're treating me?' she asked with a cool smile.

He shook his head.

'I know I asked for that but, no. I'm referring to the arrangements you suggested for looking after Callum. We're going home now, but could you come round within the hour to take over and I'll do your evening surgery?'

'Yes, of course. I'll have to do some food shopping first,

though. Living alone doesn't exactly motivate one to keep a well-stocked larder.'

Jack smiled for the first time.

'Tell me about it!'

'Have you heard from Carla yet?' Jemima asked. 'Or is it too soon to expect a call?'

Jack shook his head, sombre once more.

'She won't be there yet. Cornwall to Scotland is a long journey.'

'How long do you think she'll be away?'

He shrugged.

'As long as it takes. Derrick's in Intensive Care.'

'Supposing he doesn't recover. What then?'

'We'll cross that bridge when we get to it.'

'We?'

'Yes, she and I.'

In other words, *she* wasn't going to be figuring in any decisions he might make. It was a strange thing that Jack should have all this concern for someone who really had betrayed him, while she herself had done nothing wrong.

Was this the same man as the one who'd treated her with frantic tenderness on the night of the accident? His face white with horror as he'd looked down at her sprawled beneath the tree branches? She was still sore from the effects of it.

Did he believe what she'd told him about Mark? If he didn't, there really was no future for them, as a relationship without trust wasn't going anywhere.

But holding a post-mortem on what she'd thought to be the love of her life wasn't going to put food into Callum's mouth, and once Jack and the child had gone she went shopping.

Callum was a good-tempered child and in no time at all he was toddling around after Jemima while she prepared his

meal. Children who'd been passed from one person to another to be cared for usually adjusted well to strangers, and
she thought that Callum was no exception.

She wanted children herself one day, but the time for
dreaming of golden-haired boys and hazel-eyed girls
seemed to have been put on hold because a child of different parentage needed the man in her life.

'More,' the hungry toddler was crying, waving his plastic
spoon.

He'd emptied the bowl of fresh vegetables and chicken
that she'd given him in record time. Putting her own needs
to one side, Jemima devoted herself to his.

He was asleep when Jack came home after evening surgery, and when he saw the table laid with his best china
and glassware, in the candlelit room, his face lightened.

'Fantastic,' he murmured as he poured himself a drink
and sank down onto the sofa. 'I can't remember when last
I came home to something like this…if ever.'

Jemima smiled as her earlier frustrations regarding him
melted away. Did he feel the rightness of it like she did?
Her face was flushed from the heat of the stove, her fine-
boned body covered by a big plastic apron, and for a second
she pretended that this was their life, her being here with
a meal ready to serve when he came home.

Tonight could be theirs. There was no ex-wife to disrupt
the moment or manipulative Mark hovering. Just the two
of them and the child sleeping upstairs.

'Are you ready to eat?' she asked.

'Yes. I'm starving.'

'Right, if you'll pour the wine, I'll dish up.'

They were more relaxed during the meal than she could
ever remember, very aware of each other but keeping it

cool and friendly. When they'd finished eating Jack said, 'Let's have our coffee by the fire.'

As she brought in the tray Jemima caught her foot in the rug by the fireplace and cream, sugar and fine china cups would have gone flying if Jack's arms hadn't come out to steady her.

That was when the spark ignited. As they gazed into each other's eyes with the tray separating them, Jack took it from her and placed it carefully on a nearby table.

Her gaze was wide and watchful and he said in a low voice, 'Have you any idea how beautiful you are, Jemima Penrose?'

She shook her head without speaking.

'Let's call a truce,' he suggested in the same quiet tone, and before she could reply he was taking her in his arms and this time as he kissed her there were no hurtful questions being asked. It was how she'd always dreamed it would be. The two of them fused together in tender desire.

Jack was holding her so close she could feel his arousal thrusting against her, and for her part her breasts were hard and aching against the solid wall of his chest.

The phone rang at that moment and they became still.

Jack groaned.

'Damn! Who can that be?'

Jemima's smile was wry.

'The only way to find out is to answer it.'

'It's the mayoress's housekeeper,' he said with a sigh after a short conversation. 'Your friend Glenda has had a fall and hurt her back. She's asking that you go round there.'

Once again the spell was broken, she thought ruefully. Were the fates trying to tell them something? She touched his downcast face gently.

'I have to go, Jack. Glenda's had major surgery on her spine and will be terrified of having done serious damage.'

He sighed. 'Of course. I'll see you tomorrow...and thanks for looking after Callum and making the lovely meal.'

'My pleasure,' she said softly and reaching her coat off the hallstand she hurried out into the winter night.

The lights of the house on the hill were blazing out across its trim lawns when Jemima arrived at the big arched doorway, and the moment she'd rung the bell the housekeeper was there beckoning for her to enter.

Glenda was lying on the floor in the hallway and as Jemima came towards her she cried out weakly, 'Is that you, Jemima, dear?'

'Yes, it's me,' she said as she bent over her. 'What happened?'

'I'd been watering my plants and some of it must have spilled onto the polished wooden floor. I stepped on it and went flying.'

'Where does it hurt?' Jemima asked.

'At the bottom of my back. In the same place that I had the surgery. I fell backwards with such a thud, Jemima,' she said shakily.

'Can you move your legs?'

'Er...yes.'

'Good. But I'm not going to risk moving you. I'm going to ring for an ambulance. They'll bring a backboard to lift you up on. We can't take any chances after what you've been through. Once they get you to A and E they'll do X-rays and we'll take it from there.'

'Did I interrupt anything by calling you out at this hour?' her friend asked.

Jemima smiled. She wasn't going to tell Glenda that

she'd been in Jack's arms when the call had come through. The feisty mayoress would be mortified.

When the paramedics had lifted Glenda into the ambulance a few minutes later, Jemima stood looking down at her. The mayoress was very pale and beads of sweat were standing out on her brow.

'Don't worry,' Jemima soothed. 'We'll have you there in no time.'

'We?' Glenda questioned.

'Yes. I'm going to come with you. I'm not leaving you until I know what the damage is.'

It was three o'clock in the morning when Jemima got home. Glenda had been X-rayed and thankfully there was no serious damage to the spine. The extreme pain had been because of the recent surgery which had left her back very tender.

Nevertheless they were keeping her in overnight and once Jemima had seen her settled in a small side ward in a less fraught state of mind, she had got in a taxi and left for home.

Hazel rang as she was eating a hasty breakfast, having slept late. In spite of the hour that she'd got back from the hospital, Jemima had found it difficult to unwind as memories of the evening spent with Jack had filled her mind once the crisis with Glenda had ended.

And now her mother was asking, 'What's going on at Jack's place? He's just been telling his father that he has the child of the awful woman he divorced staying with him.'

'Yes, that's so,' Jemima confirmed. 'Carla had to rush off to Scotland as her partner is seriously ill, and she left the boy with Jack.'

There was a pause as Hazel digested that piece of information.

'What were they doing there in the first place?' was her next question.

'Carla has left Derrick and wants to get back with Jack.'

She could hear her mother tutting at the other end of the line and Jemima had to smile. Hazel always had very definite views on how other people should run their lives, but when it came to her own...

'I think I know my stepson better than that!' she snapped.

I wish I did, Jemima thought. However, it seemed that there were other matters that her mother wished to discuss.

'Jack says that you've got your arm in a sling. That the Chimes Hotel was a casualty of erosion and that you were hurt when it happened.'

'Yes, I was,' she admitted, 'but I'm all right now and the sling will be removed shortly.'

'Why didn't you let me know?'

'We tried to get in touch but you were away.'

'Ah, yes. We've been in Paris and only got back yesterday. The next time we go away I'll make sure I leave a phone number. And now, what about Christmas? James and I wondered if you'd like to come to us. There'll be more going on in London than in Rockhaven.'

'Have you invited Jack?'

'Yes, of course, but he wouldn't commit himself.'

'Then I'd like to think about it, too, if you don't mind.'

Hazel sighed. 'What an aggravating pair you are. Here we are longing to see the two of you and you're both dithering.'

Jemima's face softened. It was comforting to know that Hazel was missing her. If only it had been like that in those desolate months after her father died. It was then that she'd needed her mother.

'I'll let you know as soon as I can,' Jemima promised, and Hazel rang off, having reluctantly agreed that they wouldn't plan anything until Jack and Jemima had been in touch.

Christmas was looming ahead as an empty void and with Jack embroiled in his ex-wife's affairs and herself with nothing to look forward to, Jemima thought that she just might go to London. But it would be a last-minute decision as there would be a surgery on the morning of Christmas Eve and she couldn't leave Jack in the lurch.

'What happened with Glenda?' Jack asked when she arrived at the practice.

Jemima gave him a brief outline of what had gone on and when she'd finished he said, 'So much for that, then. I thought that for once we were going to have some time to ourselves, but it seems as if that will be the day! My dad phoned this morning,' Jack said, changing the subject. 'I take it that Hazel did likewise?'

'Yes, she wants me to go to London for Christmas.'

'Same here. Dad is keen for me to visit them, but it isn't that easy with Callum to see to.'

'So you're expecting to be caring for him over Christmas?'

He shrugged his shoulders.

'I don't know, do I? Carla has phoned a couple of times and Derrick is still very ill. So what I'll be doing at Christmas is all very unforseeable at the moment.'

There was no softener to the effect that if things had been different he'd have wanted to spend it with her, or that it would be great for the four of them to be together in London, and she began to wonder just what did go on in his mind.

'I suppose you'll be accepting the invitation,' he said tonelessly.

'I don't know,' she said evasively. 'It all depends...'

'On what?'

She wasn't to know that after last night he couldn't think of anything he wanted to do more than spend Christmas with her. But there was Callum and his peculiar parents in the background and once he'd committed himself to anything, Jack followed it through.

He was called away at that moment and with a longer list of visits than usual to be carried out she departed into the chilly December day.

The week after that was strange. With every day that passed the festive spirit at the surgery increased, but Jemima wasn't tuned in and she sensed that Jack wasn't either.

Neither were a lot of their patients as there was a flu epidemic in Rockhaven, in spite of many of its inhabitants having had the vaccination.

But amongst the many with the fever and chest infections there were still the few with uncommon illnesses, the health problems that a GP had to pass on to higher levels, and Kendrick Taylor was one of those affected.

In his late forties, the tall, bespectacled Cornishman had presented himself some time previously with symptoms of anaemia. He had been pale and listless, and from his notes Jemima had seen that he had little resistance to infection. Whatever virus was going around, he seemed to pick it up.

It had transpired that he'd worked in Africa for some years as a civil servant and she'd asked if he'd ever had malaria.

Kendrick had eyed her in surprise.

'Yes. I had a bout of it,' he replied. 'But why do you ask?'

'Sometimes those sorts of illnesses have far-reaching effects,' she'd told him. 'We'll do some blood tests and see what comes up.'

The results of the blood analysis had prompted her to send him to hospital for further tests and today he was back, looking just as peaky and twice as concerned as on his previous visits.

'The doctor at the hospital was talking about something called hypersplenism,' he said. 'My spleen is overactive and enlarged, and it's destroying my blood cells...it's a legacy from the malaria. That's why you asked me about it, isn't it?'

Jemima's glance had been on the consultant's report on the desk in front of her, which corroborated what the man was saying, but now she looked up.

'Yes. I did wonder if your spleen was just a bit too busy for your own good.'

'They're going to treat the underlying cause, but if that doesn't work it will have to come out,' he concluded gloomily, 'and I don't relish the thought of that.'

'Try not to worry too much,' she told him. 'A splenectomy isn't that serious an operation and losing your spleen won't cause any health problems. In fact, it would be more likely to remove them.'

When he'd gone, looking slightly more cheerful, Jemima found herself facing yet another flu sufferer and so the morning went on, with Jack and Bethany just as busy.

When Jack went to pick Callum up on the Friday afternoon of the weekend before Christmas, he watched the little boy's face light up at the sight of him, and as he swung him up into his arms his thoughts were in confusion.

Far away in Scotland there was a sick man who was the

boy's father. Obviously he cared for his son as he was the one who'd been facing up to his responsibilities, not Carla.

She was the unreliable one, as he well knew. But although she hadn't shown much concern for husband and son when she'd first come to Rockhaven, when she'd heard about Draycott's life-threatening condition she'd been frantic, so maybe there was some affection there after all.

Jack had a feeling that Draycott had thrown her out for some reason, and with the brazen cheek that was so much a part of her she'd decided to turn up on *his* doorstep.

What was going on between the two of them was their own business, but the child in his arms was a different matter, and the sooner a more stable lifestyle was sorted out for him the better.

The present situation couldn't go on for ever, but for the time being he was going to have to put up with it, or there could be more disruption for Callum.

Jemima's help had made a difference and he was grateful…in more ways than one. Not only would the little one be tucked up for the night each time he arrived home after evening surgery, but having Callum there brought Jemima into his orbit even more, even though after that first time she hadn't stayed to eat with them for some reason best known to herself.

But the days were going by and if something didn't happen soon he would have to start thinking about making a Christmas for Callum, and there was no way he could ask Jemima to pass up the chance of spending it amongst the bright lights of London with her mother.

Jemima had told Hazel that she would be happy to spend Christmas with them and that she would travel by train.

She was reconciled to the fact that Jack wouldn't be

there. Callum was still with him and so far there'd been no word from Carla to indicate any change of circumstances.

If he had asked her to stay, she would have done, but when she'd told him that she'd made her mind up and was leaving in the late morning of Christmas Eve, he'd merely said, 'Fine. You'll be back on the day after Boxing Day, I take it, as the sick of Rockhaven will still be here, needing our attention.'

'Yes, of course I'll be back by then,' she'd said. 'In a way it hardly seems worth going, but I've given my word and my mother and James will be disappointed if I change my mind. What about Callum and you? If he isn't back with his parents by then, what will you do?'

'The best I can.'

'Why don't you bring him with you?' she'd suggested casually.

It was one way she would see Jack over Christmas if he did, but he'd shaken his head.

'If his mother comes for him she needs to find him here…and our parents have only a limited number of bedrooms.'

He was making excuses, she'd thought. Being with her wasn't as high on his list of priorities as being with him was on hers, and that had been the end of the discussion.

And so the twenty-fourth of December found Jemima heading for the bright lights of London with little enthusiasm. Her mother and James were at the station to meet her, and when she saw them her spirits rose.

At least they wanted her company, were glad to see her, and she would have been happy to put Jack out of her mind if he hadn't been the one topic of conversation as a taxi took them to Great Cumberland Place where James and Hazel had a third-floor apartment.

'I'm disappointed that Jack can't be with us,' James said wistfully as Marble Arch reared up in front of them, 'but he has always had a mind of his own, and scruples to go with it.'

'It's a bit much that Jack should be left holding the baby, so to speak,' Hazel remarked tartly. She turned to Jemima. 'Surely he doesn't still have feelings for this Carla woman?'

'I'm sure I don't know,' Jemima said uncomfortably, aware that the man in question wouldn't be pleased to hear himself discussed like that.

'I suggested that he bring Callum with him,' she told them, 'but he wouldn't hear of it. Jack said that he wanted to be there if Carla came for him.'

'I can't disagree with that,' Hazel remarked, still on her high horse. 'James and I aren't running a crèche.'

It was no use. Jemima had to defend him. 'How many unattached men do you know who would give up their Christmas to look after someone else's child and pass up the chance of being with their family to do so?'

James patted her hand in the gloom of the taxi.

'Not many, Jemima. Your mother and I are lucky in our children, and Jack is fortunate to have such a champion in you.'

Hazel had turned her head away. There was a satisfied smile on her face and Jemima had a feeling that she'd just been manoeuvred into making a declaration of some sort.

The apartment was elegant and spacious—a total contrast to Surf Cottage with its nooks and crannies, smooth old wood and rose-washed walls, which went to show just how much her mother must have fretted there.

She and James had booked seats for a musical at one of the London theatres, and as Jemima dressed for the occasion she thought wistfully, that this would be perfect if Jack were here. Without him it meant nothing.

But she nevertheless put on a smiling face for their parents and prepared to play her part. And whenever the vision of a small child banging a plastic bowl and shouting 'More!' came to mind, she put it firmly to one side.

They went for a meal after the show, amongst the dazzling Christmas lights and huge decorated spruces that seemed to be everywhere.

There was a buzz in the atmosphere, gaiety everywhere, and windswept seafronts with the mighty Atlantic pushing up against them seemed a million miles away.

It was late when they got back and her mother and James went straight to bed, but Jemima wasn't ready for sleep and she sat by the window, staring out onto the London street which, even at that hour, was still busy with traffic and late night revellers.

Christmas Day had already arrived. What had Santa Claus got in his sack for her? she wondered. Even as she asked the question, she had the answer.

There was no gift-wrapping or glitter. Just a man getting out of a four-wheel-drive in the street below. Tall, well proportioned, the streetlamps glinting on hair of pale gold. As if he sensed her amazed gaze on him, he looked up and Jemima's world righted itself.

She was there waiting for him as the lift spilled out its occupants on the third floor of the apartments, her eyes huge with surprise, her heart beating like a drum, and it was only Jack's cool 'Hello, there, Jemima' that stopped her from throwing herself into his arms.

'Hello, yourself,' she breathed. 'How does this come about?'

'Carla turned up on my doorstep late afternoon, wanting to take her son home to Scotland in time for Christmas.'

'Did you know she was coming?'

'No, of course not. That isn't her style. Apparently Draycott is well on the mend and desperate to see the boy. And wait for it…so was she, believe it or not.'

'Just like that!'

'Mmm. But she didn't get away without a lecture from yours truly. I've told her that Callum has to come first. That I shall be keeping my eye on them and if I have any doubts about his welfare she'll be hearing from me and others.'

Jack was looking around him.

'So which of these prestigious dwellings is our parents' love nest?'

'Follow me,' she said, and led the way with a new spring in her step.

CHAPTER TEN

CHRISTMAS DAY was a mixture of pain and pleasure as far as Jemima was concerned.

Hazel and James had appeared the night before at the sound of Jack's voice, and the four of them had stayed up until the early hours, chatting.

The older couple had been delighted that he'd made it and, typical of Hazel, she'd wanted to know what he'd done with Callum.

'Gave him back to his mother,' Jack had told her smoothly. 'Carla has taken Callum to Scotland to see his father.'

'And is she likely to be coming back?' she'd asked.

'That remains to be seen.'

Jemima's spirits had dropped. She'd thought they'd seen the last of Jack's ex-wife, but maybe not.

They all exchanged gifts on Christmas morning and Jemima was mortified that she had nothing to give him. There was a present—she'd bought him a cashmere sweater the colour of his eyes—but it was back at the cottage.

She'd hesitated about giving it to him before she'd left for London. And now, here he was, most welcome but totally unexpected, and she had nothing to give him.

As Hazel and James unwrapped the presents from their respective children, Jack drew Jemima towards the mistletoe and once she was underneath he kissed her lightly and put a small package in her hand.

The brilliance of her smile when she saw the jade bracelet inside put the winter sun to shame. But like that sphere, it soon faded when he said, 'Just to say thanks for the way you've settled in at the practice and for helping me with Callum.'

So there wasn't anything personal about the gift, she thought dismally as she looked down on it.

'I have something for you, but it's back at the cottage,' she told him. 'I wasn't expecting to see you here.'

He shrugged.

'No problem. I wasn't expecting to see myself here, but I am, and I suggest we make the most of the next two days as we'll have to arrange a dawn start the day after.'

'Meaning?'

'Let's forget our cares and differences for a while and be at peace with each other.'

Jemima stared at him. That was good! She wasn't the one with the hang-ups. Her only problem was the lifeboat. The mere thought of it brought back the terrifying images that of late she'd been able to push away.

He saw her expression and asked, 'What's wrong? Don't you want that for us?'

'Of course I do,' she said flatly, 'But amongst our cares and differences, as you describe them, is the lifeboat—and I don't think I'll ever be able to come to terms with what happened.'

Jemima's voice trailed away as she watched the light die out of Jack's eyes and he said sombrely, 'I know. But did you have to bring it up today of all days? If you remember, I was on the point of asking them to find another GP to answer the call-outs, but you were at pains to tell me to stay with them, even though the thought of it gives you the horrors. Maybe one day I'll understand the workings of your mind, Jemima, but as yet that day hasn't dawned.'

On that note he went to talk to his father and Hazel, and Jemima was left with the uncomfortable feeling that she had unintentionally put the blight on what might have been a day to treasure.

After lunch they all watched TV for a while and then played Scrabble, and all the time Jemima was overwhelmingly conscious of Jack seated beside her, his thigh only inches from hers, the hands with the magic touch reaching out to the board to complete yet another word, and the cool withdrawn glance that was keeping her at a distance more efficiently than any barbed-wire fence.

She was hemmed in by circumstance, Jemima thought as the afternoon wore on. If it wasn't for hurting her mother and James, and that there would be few trains to Cornwall on Christmas Day, she would have gone home.

When she'd seen Jack in the street below the night before, she'd been filled with delight, but she should have known that nothing in life was ever as one expected it to be.

It was when she came up with a nine-letter word that she had his attention for the first time since their earlier sparring, and as their glances held briefly, his father said laughingly, 'Well done, Jemima. But I do hope that you're not trying to tell us something with the word ''miserable''.'

'No, of course not,' she assured him with a weak smile, hoping that a certain person at the table *might* be wondering if there was a message in it for him.

They'd been to a candlelit carol service at a nearby church and then come back for the meal that their parents had prepared, and all the time Jemima had been thinking that this was their first Christmas together and it should have been fantastic instead of lukewarm.

She'd noticed her mother observing her with a watchful eye and wondered what she was thinking. As they cleared away after the meal, leaving the two men chatting companionably in the sitting room, she was about to find out.

'Don't you get on with Jack?' Hazel asked as they stacked the dishwasher.

'Yes, of course. Why do you ask?'

'I'm a lot of things,' her mother said, 'but I'm not blind. You make a striking pair. Why don't you do something about it?'

Jemima felt warm colour wash up in her face.

'We *are* a striking pair,' she admitted with a wry smile, 'but not quite in the way you meant it. The blows we inflict on each other are verbal rather than physical, but they hurt just as much.'

Hazel sighed.

'So it's not a love match, then? Because I've seen the way he looks at you and it's not the same as with any other woman I've seen him with.'

'That's because we're both doctors—work colleagues. He's bound to see me differently,' she said lightly.

The last thing she needed was her mother to start zooming into her private affairs. Her relationship with Jack was already a disaster, but with Hazel on her case it would go from bad to worse.

'Mmm, I suppose so,' Hazel agreed reluctantly, and to Jemima's relief that was the end of it.

Boxing Day dawned mild and dry, and after breakfast Jack suggested a walk in Hyde Park. James was about to agree when a meaningful look from his wife made him change his mind.

'We'll have a rest if you don't mind,' Hazel said, 'but I'm sure that Jemima will be missing the sea breezes and would welcome some fresh air.'

'Is that so?' he asked levelly.

'I don't mind a walk,' she said easily.

It would appear that her mother was still plotting, she

thought wryly. But Hazel was wasting her time and when the chance arose she would tell her not to speak about her as if she wasn't there, that she was quite capable of making up her own mind.

Yet was she? She was like a vessel drifting at sea where Jack Trelawney was concerned, rudderless, non-functioning and listing towards no sane conclusion.

As they walked amongst the London crowds, tempted out by the sun like themselves, they were both silent. Jemima was staring straight ahead, dressed in high-heeled boots and with arms swinging free now that the sling wasn't needed any more. Her long wool coat of terracotta made the pale skin of her face look ethereal against the glowing brown of her hair.

The man by her side, dressed more casually in a black leather jacket and grey trousers, was too aware of his companion to take any notice of the attention they were attracting.

Ever since she'd mentioned the lifeboat on Christmas Day, he'd been in the doldrums. There was no way he would ever want to minimise Jemima's horror and grief over what had happened to her father, but life had to go on, and at the moment neither of them were prepared to admit that they had a future together.

Hazel was up to something. He could tell. But she was going to be disappointed. Jemima and he weren't going anywhere. His bones melted whenever he thought about the times he'd held her in his arms, but he'd been wary of mentioning the word 'love' and so had she. It was a sick situation if there was only lust to keep them fretting for each other.

'So, what profound conclusions have you come to?' Jemima asked, suddenly breaking into the silence.

'About what?'

'Us.'

'Why? Should I be coming to conclusions? The word has a final sound to it.'

'Exactly.'

'So you're saying that we should call it a day.'

'We're getting nowhere, are we?'

'What do you want of me, Jemima?'

'Just some trust and understanding.'

'And you think you're not getting that?'

'I can't believe you need to ask. Your insensitivity amazes me.'

'Really!' Jack said, in a voice as cutting as a knife edge. 'Then we make a good pair, with my insensitivity and your mean spirit.'

That brought Jemima to a halt.

'Am I to take it that we're on about the lifeboat again?'

'If the cap fits.'

'I see. Well, thanks for being so understanding. I'll try to be as supportive for you when you lose someone dear to you.'

I just have, he thought wretchedly. He'd let Jemima goad him into saying the unforgivable thing and there was no-where to go from there.

'You might as well let me drive you home in the morning instead of taking the train,' he said stiffly, later that night.

Jemima shook her head.

'No, thanks. I'd rather use my ticket, and it's a more relaxing way to travel.'

'Than with me, you mean?' he said in a low voice.

'If the cap fits,' she said sweetly.

It was January with its cold winds and driving rain. The lifeboat had been called out a few times since Christmas but Jack hadn't been needed and each time Jemima's sick fear had gradually subsided.

Since their disastrous walk through Hyde Park they had been polite but distant with each other, with no contact outside the practice.

Jemima had asked about Callum a few days after their return from London, and Jack had said levelly, 'Draycott is home now. He and Carla are reconciled and hopefully Callum's home life will be more stable from now on.'

His voice had been totally expressionless so she'd had to make a guess as to whether he was pleased or sorry about the reconciliation, but common sense said that a man as inflexible as Jack Trelawney wouldn't make the same mistake twice.

She'd seen him walking the headland and the seafront a few times between surgeries and in the evenings, a tall, remote figure silhouetted against grey skies and restless water, and had prayed for the Cornish spring to come, when the beauty of Rockhaven might be some solace for her gloom.

As the winds continued to blow and the heavens spill forth, Jemima found herself driving along the seafront on a Sunday afternoon.

She'd been to see Glenda and had shared afternoon tea with the mayoress, who had fortunately recovered from the fall with no disastrous results.

It had been the first time they'd socialised since the night that she'd sent for Jemima, and Glenda had been bringing her up to date on the state of the cliff and the misfortunes of those who'd owned the ill-fated hotel.

The mayoress had called at the surgery a couple of times after she'd been discharged from hospital, but today had been the first time they'd met in a relaxed manner.

'So, how are you and Jack Trelawney getting along?'

Glenda asked. 'After seeing you both at my ball, I've been expecting an announcement of some sort.'

Jemima sighed.

'I do have an announcement. It's off. That is, if it was ever on.'

'You're crazy, the pair of you,' she hooted. 'What's the problem?'

'It's more a case of what isn't. The man is a law unto himself. He accused me of having slept with Mark Emmerson, for one thing. Not that it's any of his business if I had, and even when I'd convinced him that I hadn't, we were still at odds with each other. But the final thrust that cut more deeply than anything was when he told me I was mean-spirited because I couldn't cope with him going out on the lifeboat.'

'We all say stupid things when we're miserable and frustrated,' Glenda said placatingly. 'You have to remember that Jack hasn't had much luck with relationships in the past. Why don't you go to him and make up? If ever I saw a man in love it was he on the night of the ball, and he doesn't strike me as the fickle type.

'Promise me that you'll have another try to make a go of it before you give up on him,' she urged later when Jemima was leaving, and Jemima nodded gloomily.

As she drove down the hillside from Glenda's place, she wished she hadn't promised to seek Jack out, but she had, and the sooner the better, so that she could see what lay ahead more clearly.

But not today. Tomorrow would be soon enough.

They were about to launch the inflatable 'D' class lifeboat as she drove along the seafront in driving rain, and her hands gripped the steering-wheel more tightly.

As she slowed down, ready to turn into the side street

near the lifeboat house, Bill Stennet appeared beside the
car, motioning for her to roll down the window.

'I need a favour, Jemima,' he said urgently. 'The coastguards have called us out. We have a casualty who's injured, unconscious by the sound of it, and is cut off by a
mischievous tide. We need a doctor on board.'

Jemima felt her mouth go dry and the colour drain from
her face. She shook her head.

'You'll have to get hold of Jack. That's his territory.'

'I can't,' Bill said as raindrops dripped off his cap. 'He's
the casualty.'

'What?' Jemima cried as she swerved out of the line of
traffic and parked by the kerbside.

'How? Why? Where?' she asked as she flung the car
door open.

He took her arm.

'I'll tell you when we're on board. There's no time to
lose. We're taking the D-class because the strip of sand
where he's marooned isn't big enough for the Severn to
beach.'

'Jemima!' one of the helmsmen cried when he saw her.
'This is like old times.'

She managed a wan smile and began to throw on the
waterproofs that were waiting for her, all the time sick with
dread that history was going to repeat itself. Her own fear
had been wiped out by her concern for Jack and now all
she wanted was to find him.

What was he doing in such a position? she wondered
raggedly as the boat cut through the waves. He knew the
coastline well enough and was the last person to do something as stupid as getting cut off by the tide. And he was
a strong swimmer, but an unconscious man couldn't swim,
could he?

If he was spared she would spend the rest of her life in

gratitude, she thought frantically. It wouldn't matter if they never got it right, just as long as he was there, somewhere in the world…and not in a watery grave.

As if in answer to her fraught imaginings, Bill came up beside her and, shouting to be heard above the wind, he said, 'From what the coastguards tell us, Jack was out walking along the coast. And a few miles out of Rockhaven he came upon a pair of eleven-year-old lads who'd been messing about on the beach in a little sandy cove and hadn't noticed that the tide was surrounding them. Their only escape was up a steep rock face and they were too frightened to try. The lads have told the coastguards that Jack went down to them and began to help them up to safety, but when they were past the worst and he was bringing up the rear, a boulder came rattling down and knocked him off his feet.

'When they looked down he was lying on the beach, not moving, with the tide coming ever nearer. Fortunately they had the sense to run to the coastguard post for help and they contacted us.'

Jemima could taste salt on her lips as she listened. Salt from the sea mingling with salt from the tears that were spilling down her cheeks.

It was just the kind of thing Jack would do, she thought. He loved children. It had been obvious from the way he'd cared for Callum when he wasn't responsible for him in any way, and he would have been determined that the two eleven-year-olds weren't going to drown if he could help it. And now…now he might be going to die himself.

'Faster!' she cried. 'Can't we go any faster?'

'We're doing a full twenty knots,' Bill shouted back. 'If he hasn't been washed away we should come upon him any second.'

Suddenly it was there, a small patch of golden sand below a sheer rock face, and the three men and Jemima were straining their eyes to see Jack.

'I have him!' Bill cried as he brought the scene closer through binoculars. 'We have a matter of minutes to get to him. Beach the boat the second we get there,' he ordered. 'Jemima'll need to have a look at him before we try to move him.'

He glanced at her pale face. 'And, Jemima,' he added sombrely, 'I hope you're prepared for the worst if it has happened.'

No! I'm not! she wanted to cry, but knew he was right. A fall from such a height on such terrain could easily be fatal, and if that was the case she would want to die, too.

The tide was strong and dangerous and they had difficulty trying to beach the craft. Precious seconds were being lost and Jemima cried, 'I'll get out and swim to him with a line.'

Bill shook his head.

'That's our job, Jemima. Yours is to treat him when we get to him.'

'Yes! Exactly!' she shrieked. 'And that's what Jack is desperately in need of…medical help. And I'm the one you've brought along for that purpose, so I'm going to him.' And without waiting for an answer, she jumped overboard and began to swim with the tide.

When Jemima felt her feet on sand she rushed over to the still, dark shape that was the man she loved, and before doing anything else fixed the line that she'd brought with her onto him. If a wave were to come and wash him away while she was examining him, at least the crew would be able to pull him back.

To her immense relief there was a pulse and a heartbeat. But Jack's face was blue with cold beneath the blood that the wind had dried on it, and his eyes were tightly closed. At least he was breathing, she thought thankfully.

All his limbs seemed to be at the right angles too, so she could only pray that there was no internal damage. If there was, there was nothing she could do about it out here, except make sure that the lifeboat men handled him carefully.

Now that she could actually see him and touch him, her fear was lessening, but there was a long way to go. The inflatable had managed to beach this time and with only seconds to spare they were ready to take Jack on board.

As she crouched in the bottom of the boat with him, supporting him against her, the crew tried to take off from the fast disappearing strip of sand, but each time the boat was swamped by the huge waves and it was only at the fifth attempt that they managed to get out to sea again, having sustained some damage to the propeller which fortunately didn't seem to affect progress.

When they reached the harbour a cheer went up from those waiting, and as if the noise had penetrated his unconsciousness Jack opened his eyes.

To see the bright blue of them eyeing her blankly from the bottom of the boat was a moment of pure joy for Jemima, and then he was asking croakily, 'Where have *you* come from, Jemima?'

'She's been doing your job, my son,' the elderly coxswain told him with a chuckle. 'And right determined she was that you weren't going to feed the fishes.'

The casualty groaned and she didn't know if it was in pain or dismay, but she didn't care. Jack was alive. The next thing they had to do was get him to hospital and then, God willing, she might get the chance to tell him that she loved him.

When the doctor in A and E came to her he said with a smile, 'Jack Trelawney is a cool customer and he must have a skull like cast iron. He tells me that in the split second after the rock, or whatever it was, hit him, he arched himself away from the cliffside, thereby falling through space instead of bouncing off the rocks as he fell. And, of course, he landed on sand which, no doubt, explains why he's got off so lightly.'

'But he was unconscious when we got to him,' she said unbelievingly. 'How could he not have been hurt to be in that state?'

'The blow to the head, of course, and the impact as he hit the ground, but amazingly there are no haematomas presenting themselves or fractures of the skull. Cuts and bruises, yes, but he'll survive those. And by the way, he's asking for you. They've just taken him up to a small private ward on the first floor.'

Jemima took a deep breath. She would know when she saw him if it was the right moment. A quick glance in a nearby mirror told her that she wasn't looking her best, with hair damp and lustreless from the sea water, face white, still with the aftermath of terror on it, and her legs almost giving way when she got to her feet. But she didn't care. Whatever *she* looked like, *he* would look worse.

When she went in Jack was sitting up, his gaze fixed on the open doorway. Jemima hoped that she was the one he was waiting for.

It seemed as if she might be.

'Jemima!' he breathed as she reached his side. 'Are you all right?'

'I should be asking you that,' she said with a smile.

He shook his head.

'No! No way! I can't believe that you put your fear to one side because of me, especially after what I said. You should have let me drown.'

'And spend the rest of my life in misery without you?' she said lightly, and then took a deep breath. This was the moment. She was going to jump in at the deep end and if he didn't respond she would want to crawl away into the nearest hole.

'Having seen the care you're prepared to give to the off-spring of others, I can only imagine how you would cherish our children,' she went on in the same tone.

His battered face went blank.

'I think that the knock on the head might have affected my hearing,' he said softly. 'Would you mind saying that again?'

Jemima took his hand in hers.

'You heard it the first time, my devious one. I love you, Jack Trelawney, and if you'll have me I will never ever leave you. You'll be stuck with me for ever.' Her voice broke. 'But, please, if you don't want me, tell me quickly. Put me out of my misery.'

He held out his arms.

'Want you! Want you, Jemima Penrose! I hunger for you every minute of the day. When I was lying on that beach I didn't care whether I was rescued or not, so fed up was I…and then what happened? My beautiful Jemima took her courage in both hands and came looking for me. I'll re-member that for as long as I live. You saved my life.'

'Not entirely on my own,' she said softly. 'Bill and the others did their bit.'

'Yes, but if it had been their faces looking down at me as I lay in the bottom of the inflatable I might have doubted whether they'd done me a favour,' Jack said with a quiz-zical smile. 'I love and adore you, Jemima. How soon can we be married and start having those babies that you want to see me with?'

'Soon,' she promised from the shelter of his arms. 'but

I can't guarantee how long it will take my mother to decide on a wedding outfit.'

It was the day that they were to be married in the tiny church on the seafront where she and her father had worshipped. Jemima had never set foot in it since his death, but now she felt differently.

She had faced up to her fears and triumphed because of her love for another special man, and today she was going to make the vows that would bind her to him for ever.

James was to give her away, and a delighted Glenda was to be her matron of honour.

Hazel hadn't been too keen on the idea. She'd thought the mayoress too old. But as she was pleased about everything else regarding her daughter's marriage to her stepson, she hadn't made too big a fuss.

And when the moment came and a hush fell over the tiny church because the bride was on its threshold, Jemima knew that the prodigal daughter had come home…in every way.

The man who loved her more than life itself was waiting for her inside, and it was with that knowledge that she began to walk towards him in radiance.

Modern Romance™
...seduction and
passion guaranteed

Tender Romance™
...love affairs that
last a lifetime

Sensual Romance™
...sassy, sexy and
seductive

Blaze
...sultry days and
steamy nights

Medical Romance™
...medical drama on
the pulse

Historical Romance™
...rich, vivid and
passionate

MILLS & BOON®

Winner at

2001 **IDEA** INTERNATIONAL
DESIGN
EFFECTIVENESS
AWARDS

MAT5

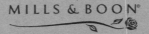

Medical Romance™

A VERY SINGLE WOMAN *by Caroline Anderson*

Dr Nick Lancaster didn't understand why a beautiful, talented doctor like Helen Moore would want to come to remote Suffolk to work part-time and adopt and raise a child as her own. He had to find out why she'd mothballed her emotions – because she'd blasted all his into the open and raised his masculine instincts for the first time in years!

THE STRANGER'S SECRET *by Maggie Kingsley*

When Greensay Island's only doctor, Jess Arden, broke her leg, she wanted to go on practising but knew she couldn't manage. Then the island's recluse, Ezra Dunbar, revealed himself to be a doctor. Why hadn't he been using his medical skills? And, until he confided his secrets, should Jess be dreaming of their future together?

HER PARTNER'S PASSION *by Carol Wood*

When Dr Abbie Scott returns home from America she discovers a sexy stranger in her home. Whether she likes it or not, Dr Caspar Darke is her new partner and he's here to stay! And living and working together, day and night, makes her aware of how dangerously irresistible he is…

On sale 7th June 2002

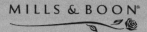

Medical Romance™

THE OUTBACK MATCH by *Lucy Clark*

To the people of Heartfield Dr Halley Ryan is the enemy – sent to close their hospital. And even if they can be won over by her natural friendliness, Dr Max Pearson will not let his feelings towards her be more than professional. He has a secure future mapped out with his fiancée… so why does his heart tell him he's engaged to the wrong woman?

THE PLAYBOY DOCTOR by *Sarah Morgan*

Hardworking and dedicated, Dr Joanna Weston was everything she believed her new locum Seb Macaulay wasn't. Every woman he met adored him and Joanna was determined to be the exception. Little by little Seb's warmth broke down her protective barriers and she began to fall in love with him. But he could so easily break her heart…

CHALLENGING DR BLAKE by *Rebecca Lang*

Working on dangerous assignments had taught World Aid nurse Signy Clover never to develop emotional bonds with anybody. Meeting Dr Dan Blake in the wilderness of Western Canada nearly changed her mind, but she fought their mutual attraction at every step. Winning Signy's love would be the biggest challenge of Dan's life!

On sale 7th June 2002

0702/73/MB38

Coming in July

⬥⟞⟨◈⟩⟝⬥

The Ultimate Betty Neels Collection

⬥⟞⟨◈⟩⟝⬥

✳ A stunning 12 book collection beautifully packaged for you to collect each month from bestselling author Betty Neels.

✳ Loved by millions of women around the world, this collection of heartwarming stories will be a joy to treasure forever.

Available at most branches of WH Smith,
Tesco, Martins, Borders, Eason, Sainsbury's
and most good paperback bookshops.

MILLS & BOON®

heat *of the* night

LORI FOSTER
GINA WILKINS
VICKI LEWIS THOMPSON

3 SIZZLING SUMMER NOVELS

*Available at most branches of WH Smith,
Tesco, Martins, Borders, Eason, Sainsbury's
and most good paperback bookshops.*

FREE!

2 Books
and a surprise gift!

We would like to take this opportunity to thank you for reading this Mills & Boon® book by offering you the chance to take TWO more specially selected titles from the Medical Romance™ series absolutely FREE! We're also making this offer to introduce you to the benefits of the Reader Service™—

- ★ FREE home delivery
- ★ FREE gifts and competitions
- ★ FREE monthly Newsletter
- ★ Books available before they're in the shops
- ★ Exclusive Reader Service discount

Accepting these FREE books and gift places you under no obligation to buy; you may cancel at any time, even after receiving your free shipment. Simply complete your details below and return the entire page to the address below. ***You don't even need a stamp!***

YES! Please send me 2 free Medical Romance books and a surprise gift. I understand that unless you hear from me, I will receive 4 superb new titles every month for just £2.55 each, postage and packing free. I am under no obligation to purchase any books and may cancel my subscription at any time. The free books and gift will be mine to keep in any case.

M2ZEB

Ms/Mrs/Miss/Mr ....Initials...

BLOCK CAPITALS PLEASE

Surname...

Address...

....

....Postcode ....

Send this whole page to:
UK: The Reader Service, FREEPOST CN81, Croydon, CR9 3WZ
EIRE: The Reader Service, PO Box 4546, Kilcock, County Kildare (stamp required)